£2.50

# The Doom of Soulis

*Also by Moira Miller*

Did You Think I Would Leave You Crying?

MOIRA MILLER

# The Doom
# of Soulis

Methuen

First published 1987
by Methuen Children's Books Ltd
11 New Fetter Lane, London EC4P 4EE
Copyright © 1987 Moira Miller
Printed in Great Britain

British Library Cataloguing in Publication Data

Miller, Moira
  The doom of Soulis.
  I. Title
  823' .914[F]      PZ7

  ISBN 0-416-02422-X

Printed in Great Britain by
Redwood Burn Limited, Trowbridge, Wiltshire

# Contents

*Author's Note*

The Doom of Soulis is based on a
Scottish legend of the Fourteenth
Century. Of the characters, only
the king, Robert the Bruce, and
Soulis, Lord of Liddesdale, were
known to have existed.

The castle of Hermitage still stands,
a bleak and eerie ruin at the head
of Liddesdale on the Scottish Border.

## One

*'There will come a time...'*

The shade beneath the oak trees was cool in the stifling noonday heat. Sunlight flickered through a gently stirring canopy of leaves. The birds had long since fallen asleep in the shimmering heat, and even the river, running low after long dry summer weeks, whispered over the smooth stones. In the deepest shade, where the trees grew lush by the river bank, a man lay, unmoving, the wind hardly stirring the long dark hair and grey-flecked beard. One strong brown hand curled limply round a small, curiously patterned coffer that lay hidden beneath the folds of his faded blue robe.

Around him the little wood held its breath, the only sound the steady, gentle snore of Thomas the Seannachie – storyteller and rhymer.

A squirrel, swinging lazily from branch to branch, dropped an acorn which fell with a thud, soft and sudden as a startled heartbeat, by the man's head. He sighed and turned on his side, hazy eyes half open, squinting through the long grass at the deserted sunlit clearing, uncovering the coffer.

It was a small box, the wood worn black and shining by the hands of generations past. There were those who said it came from the ancient lost dynasties of the great Kings of Egypt, others who had heard tell that Moses had borne it with him on the Long March to the Promised Land. Still others swore that the Devil had had a hand in the creation of the coffer. The rumours were rife, though very few had actually seen it. Thomas was careful of that. Now, half-remembering an uneasy dream, he pulled his robe across to hide the box again and settled to sleep.

The harsh cry brought him fully and instantly awake.

Sparrows and blackbirds, twittering in alarm, fled from the treetops. A huge black and white bird flapped noisily down through the leaves to perch on the rotting trunk of a fallen tree. The slackness of sleep cleared from his face as Thomas pulled himself warily up on to an elbow to face that wicked, shining eye.

'Good morrow Master Magpie.' He nodded almost courteously.

The bird fixed him with a long, calculating stare, shifting closer along the trunk. Thomas reached, slowly, carefully, towards the stout staff which lay in the long grass by his side.

10

As his fingers closed around the wood their eyes held for several seconds, each studying the other, then with a sudden mocking shout the bird spread black, gleaming wings and swooped off into the trees.

A cloud seemed to pass across the sun.

The Seannachie shivered and pulled himself stiffly to his knees.

'Well met, old man, well met indeed!'

Thomas had heard no man come or go in the wood that day, and yet now before him stood a slim figure in a long black woollen cloak which covered him from shoulder to foot. He was young and tall, with a thin white, clever face, and hair black and shining, except for a strange streak of white above his left temple.

'Well met indeed!' The voice was soft and well-spoken, a man of quality, obviously, The Seannachie came to his feet, head bowed, leaning heavily on his staff. He seemed to make himself older and weaker in the presence of the young man.

'If you say so, my lord, if you say so.' He moved slowly. Around him the blue robe fell in heavy folds, encircling and hiding the coffer.

The younger man stepped forward. Sunlight gleamed on the shining hair and drowned in the depth of black eyes, untouched by the smile on his thin lips. He walked softly round Thomas, delicate as a hunting cat.

11

'Well met indeed, Seannachie, as I see you to be by your robe. Your fame travels before you from the taverns of Edinburgh and the homesteads of the Borders. Now perhaps you will do me the honour of accepting my humble hospitality? In return I ask only that you share your gifts of ballad and song for an evening.'

No invitation this, but an order. There was steel behind the arrogant, confident smile and the elegant mocking bow.

'Alas, my lord,' the Seannachie bowed low in return. 'You do me too much honour. But I fear I must decline your hospitality.'

The smile on the thin lips faded.

'Decline. Decline, Sir Rhymer? What possible enchantments might lure you from the hospitality of Hermitage?'

In the pause between them the Seannachie felt the hair on the back of his neck prickle, his skin suddenly thinner, the nerve endings exposed to danger. He nodded, as if confirming to himself the answer to a question, but his reply came cool and unruffled.

'I am bidden to these parts, my lord, by young Wat Scott of Branxholm Tower, and his father the old duke. Therefore, I say again, I must decline.'

The young man frowned, accustomed as he was to instant obedience. A flash of irritation, and something more, perhaps puzzlement, sparked in his eyes. This rhyming fool must be simple

12

indeed to defy him – knowing who he was.

Suddenly, unexpectedly, he smiled, with a dangerous charm that lit the sombre face.

'What Master Seannachie? The duke and young Wat is it? A nursemaid's tales for that clodhopping farmer? Bread and milksops before bedtime for the wee laird?'

He stepped back into the sunlight, laughing.

'Forget them! Accept my hospitality and you will want for nothing. I *will* have you Master Seannachie. And I shall offer you food fit for a king, fine wines and the company of real men about you.' He threw back his cloak with a sweeping gesture, uncovering a heavy gold chain on which hung a pendant with a crest known the length and breadth of the kingdom. A fine white linen sleeve flashed, dazzling, as he raised a beckoning arm.

From the trees around them, stepping silent as shadows at his back, came a group of heavily armed men.

On each black leather tunic hung the same badge, the crest of Ranulf de Soulis, Lord of Liddesdale, Master of Hermitage, Guardian of the King's Peace, distant cousin of the King's Grace — and the only living man ever to strike fear into the deepest corners of the heart of King Robert the Bruce of Scotland.

Soulis, whose father had claimed the throne and lost it to the same King Robert who now held it so precariously. Soulis, said to be the richest man in the kingdom, though none knew the source of his wealth. Soulis, hated and feared wherever his name was whispered, from the Viking Islands of the west to the Debatable Lands of the troubled Border. Appointed Guardian to maintain peace, he had ruled his estates along that Border with fearful strength.

It was said to be no natural strength. From his earliest childhood it was known that he had scorned to set foot inside a House of God. It was whispered, behind locked doors, that his power and gold came from some evil source within the grim keep of Hermitage, that the Lord of Liddesdale was in league with the Devil himself.

Whatever the fount of that power, where Soulis had an enemy his crops failed. Where he was crossed, beasts and men died of plague and palsy. Disease touched those on whom his hatred fell. Even the king, afraid to lose his support, seemed unable to control the man. And so Soulis rode the countryside at the head of his troop, seizing whatever he wanted, destroying those who stood in his way.

And now the men of that troop stood about him, ready and waiting his command. He had trained them well. Each face was set in a mask of hard, unthinking obedience, coupled with a wariness. He kept them in thrall, as wolves around the leader of the pack.

14

Soulis, watching Thomas, permitted them to approach only so far, then snapped his fingers, laughing.

'Gibbie! My horse! Let us convey our storyteller to my humble home.'

Through the trees came a white horse, finely saddled and bridled, and led by a thin, dark-haired boy.

It was difficult to tell Gibbie's age. He was thin, fragile as a child, and yet the dark eyes were old beyond their time, and had witnessed many things unknown to any child. Standing between youth and manhood he seemed too old for the one, too young for the other. He too wore the black tunic and badge, the uniform of the men who rode with Soulis, but there was about the boy a quality that set him apart. Unlike the others he watched Soulis, not with the watchfulness of a paid servant, but with fascination and a thinly disguised contempt.

Suddenly aware of the Seannachie's curious eyes on him the boy stared back, challenging and arrogant as his master.

Thomas caught his breath. The old, uncanny feeling crept upon him. From a closed and dangerous corner of his mind the half-remembered prophesy echoed down the years.

'There will come to you a boy, capable of great good or evil. Worthy to hold the coffer, or to wreak destruction as never before . . . .'

15

Soulis caught the intensity of the look that passed between them. Pushing the boy out of the way he caught the reins from his hand.

'To Hermitage, Rhymer. I would be amused.' He swung lightly into the saddle, waving to the others to follow with Thomas.

'Come, my lord,' said the Seannachie softly, but in a voice which carried clearly to each man there. 'Would you have me disappoint our king, who even now awaits me?'

Soulis froze in mid-movement.

There would be a flogging or worse for the man who had failed to pass on to him this intelligence. His horse, sensing the current of fear, whinnied restlessly, pulling on the bit. With a burst of uncontrolled fury he hauled on the reins, and hit out wildly at Gibbie, who sank to his knees gasping in pain.

'Are you unable even to hold my horse steady, runt?' The voice was light and dangerous as thin ice. 'Perhaps your talents would be better suited to minding the rats in my dungeon?' Ignoring the boy who huddled retching in the grass, he turned in the saddle to face Thomas.

'The king you say? Our noble liege come amongst us here? For what purpose may one ask? I have heard nothing of this.'

'Then it may be he came only for pleasure, my lord.' Soulis stiffened at the acid in the other's tone, then turned to his men with a sneering laugh.

'To Branxholm? Our noble Robert, the King's Grace, chooses to dine with farmers in the byre rather than grace the table of a kinsman?'

The men laughed nervously, gratefully seizing on the change of mood. Only Gibbie stood unsmiling, a dark bruise already spreading across a face set in determined loathing.

The Seannachie turned again to Soulis.

'He is the king my lord, and I suppose may choose as it pleases him.'

'The king! Oh indeed. Heed my words man. The dignity of kingship lies uneasy on Robert de Bruce, so many years living like a hunted beast in forest and cave. This flower of chivalry may, I suppose, please himself – for now at least. But they say he has been sick of late. He cannot last for ever. You foretell the future for the gossiping biddies and farmers' wives. What of the king, Rhymer?'

'I have heard, my lord, that it is passing sickness from which he will surely recover.'

'And if not? Who then shall take his place? Can you see that? Who is there to lead us against the enemy across the Border? Tell me that Seannachie.'

'Why then, my lord, the crown must surely fall to his son. It needs no soothsayer to foretell that.'

'A drooling infant! Much good he may do us.'

'He may indeed, my lord, one day, if he were

17

able to trust in the support of strong and powerful kinsmen – such as yourself.' The Seannachie stood tall and straight now, his strange pale-blue eyes fearless and challenging. No man had ever dared to address Soulis in these tones.

Gibbie, creeping back to the edge of the clearing, stood breathless as the two faced each other. To his surprise Soulis backed off from the moment.

'Powerful,' he breathed, amused. 'Oh yes, Seannachie, I have the power.' He leaned down from the saddle above Thomas, his sweeping cloak blotting out the light, his voice a gentle murmur between them.

'I have the power, and you shall see it. It has been given to me alone, and soon all others shall know that there is no man who can hurt me; no steel that may cut; no rope that shall bind. I have the power, fool, and when the time is right. When the runes are read . . .'

He sat up suddenly in the saddle. His horse wheeled, startled as his voice echoed through the quiet wood.

'When the runes are read – why then, my rhyming fool, take heed. Take heed of Soulis!'

He waved a hand in mock salute and, spurring his horse, galloped from the clearing followed by his men. The air hung thick with the smell of trampled grass, reverberating to the echo of his presence.

18

Thomas the Seannachie slowly let out his breath. At last, after so many years, the words of his master, the old storyteller, wove like the first threads of a troubled tapestry in his memory . . .

*'When it comes to pass that the evil of your time must be faced, then it may be that your power will be strong enough. But do not use it until that time.*

*'Into your hands I now pass the coffer and the key. Guard them with your life.'*

Automatically Thomas felt for the key which hung, day and night, about his neck.

The time had been long in coming, the words almost forgotten . . .

*'Go amongst our people as a Seannachie, Thomas, as I have taught you. You will be made welcome, for the gift of song and ballad is yours. But there are darker gifts which I have seen in you. Hoard them, Thomas, hoard them, for the time will come . . .'*

The old man had lain dying in his arms as Thomas held the blue cloak, a shelter against the storm which raged about them, and strained to catch the hoarse whisper . . .

*'A king will come to this land, much troubled in mind, and snapping at his heels there follows one whose power is of the Darkness of the Six Nights of Creation. It must fall to you, Thomas, to defeat him . . .'*

*'No, master, take from me this power!'*

*'I cannot take what I did not give.'*

Thomas shuddered. Men still spoke in awe of that night of storm. He saw again in his mind's eye the bleak moorland, the ring of standing stones where the old man, half-leading, half-dragging, had taken him. He recalled the taste of rain mingling with salt tears, and the lightning crashing vivid about them in the blackness.

At the height of the storm, in one earth-shattering moment, that lightning had shattered the great central stone of the ancient ring and left him cowering in terror.

But the old man had seemed to see none of this. His spirit already turned to the last journey, he had lain smiling, as if recognising through a half-open door, the way ahead. . .

*'Farewell, Thomas. This only I can say. You will not go alone. There will be love and courage to stand by your side. And there will come one . . . there will come to you a boy capable of great good and evil. Worthy to hold the coffer . . .'*

The coffer! Thomas caught up the hem of his robe, uncovering the little chest that had lain hidden from Soulis. It was still safe. Stooping to lift it his eyes met those of Gibbie, who stood silently staring from the shadows by the edge of the clearing.

Ignoring the fading shouts of Soulis and his men, the boy stepped forward. He knelt at the Seannachie's feet and, lifting the coffer as if it had been a precious infant, he laid it gently in the outstretched arms. His fingers lingered briefly on

20

the worn symbols carved in the ancient wood, like a child struggling to read an almost forgotten lesson.

'Yes, Gibbie.' The Seannachie nodded, reading confusion and question in the dark-rimmed eyes.

The boy paused as if to speak, then shaking his head, turned and ran off. Within seconds he had vanished silently into the wood.

Thomas sighed, bowing at last to the inevitable.

'It has begun.'

Gathering himself together, and squaring his shoulders, he set his face towards the setting sun, stepping out on the path that led by river and woodland across the green rolling hills of the Border Country towards Branxholm Tower, and the king.

## Two

## 'It is but child's play'

King Robert belched fruitfully, unfastened the heavy silver buckle of his belt, and stretched out his legs under the table. A pageboy standing by his shoulder leaned forward to refill the heavy pewter goblet.

After two days spent hunting on the duke's Border estates the king felt weary, but pleasantly so. The smell of wine, sweet and spicy, mingled with the aroma of woodsmoke and roasting meat in the old, comfortable hall of Branxholm Tower. It was a smell of peace and safety.

'More fruit, Sire?' The old duke by his side waved a lazy hand across the table. The servants had cleared away the meat, and wooden bowls filled to the brim with small russet apples were set glowing and polished in the warm candlelight.

'Indeed no, my lord,' said the king. 'I have dined well at your son's board this night. He shares not only his father's skill at the chase, but his generosity as a host.'

22

He raised his goblet in a toast and nodded towards young Wat Scott, who sprawled at the other end of the table gazing dreamily into the teasing blue eyes of Marion Elliot. Marion poked Wat's arm and nodded laughing towards the king.

Wat rose, a little unsteadily, to his full height, making an extravagant bow. A few drops of wine from his goblet fell like blood on the old well-scrubbed table.

'It is much honour you do us, your Grace, to visit this our seat.' His speech was formal, exquisitely careful, and only slightly slurred. Marion ducked, giggling, under his sweeping arm. At his other side her brother Allan clapped with delight.

'I fear though, Master Scott, you had best hold fast to that seat!' chuckled the king. Laughter chimed round the table as Wat resumed his chair with studied care and dignity.

King Robert sat back and watched the company through half-shut eyes. It had been a rare day or two of peace. The hunting around Branxholm was good, and the late summer weather fine and warm enough to drive the pain from joints already stiffening after years of living in the rough, running from an enemy at last, thank God, defeated.

Around him the voices of his friends rose and fell. Jokes were exchanged, lies embellished of

23

skill in the field. Robert listened, not to the words, but to the contentment in these voices, and to the warmth of their laughter. Here, surely, he sat among friends he could trust. At peace amongst themselves, they formed a tight ring of fellowship around the throne.

So the king belched, stretched back in his chair and allowed himself the luxury of a rare moment of freedom from the constant fear that had dogged him since the early days when, as the impoverished Robert de Bruce, he had set out against all the odds to seize and hold the crown of their war-torn country.

There had been other contenders for that crown. During the darkest time the strongest of them had died in a church, bleeding on the altar steps, mortally wounded by his own hand. There were still long sleepless nights when that memory came to haunt Robert. It still drove him to church to burn yet more candles so that the blessing of their light might at last penetrate into the blackest corners of his mind, driving out the devils of superstition and fear.

But now it seemed to him at last that his position on the throne was all but secure. Through long years of fighting, his people had come to respect and recognise his genius as a leader and his ability to unite the quarrelling lords, whose arguments in the past had left the kingdom at the mercy of the enemy.

24

If only, thought Robert with a twinge of unease, if only he could hold his position until his son came of age. But that son was an infant, born to a sickly mother. Long years of imprisonment in an English jail had left her weakened and Scotland without an heir. Her release at last had given them the longed-for son who could now, even as a baby, command the loyalty of a small but powerful band of men, some of whom sat around him now. But there were others, with some claim to the throne themselves, whose loyalty he could not yet trust.

Soulis for instance.

He shuddered at the thought of this distant cousin, strong and possessed of wealth, courage and intelligence. Soulis should have been the man to stand at his shoulder, ensuring the safety of the throne. He had indeed been one of the first to swear allegiance to the new king – and yet.

Robert recalled, so vividly, that light, clear, almost mocking voice taking the oath. There were certainly none at court who trusted him.

He was hated, too, by the people. From time to time rumours came out of Liddesdale of his harshness and brutality, and worse yet of practices that chilled the blood to think of them. All hearsay of course – mere country tattle – but still.

The king knew that the day must come when he would be forced to take action. Soulis was a constant unhealed sore. But then again the old debate raged in his mind, the crown desperately needed the strength of Hermitage, the largest and most commanding of the Border castles.

Always a man of action and firm decision, Robert feared and loathed Soulis, who seemed able so completely to destroy his judgment and freeze that action.

He shivered, took a deep draught of wine and became aware with a shock that Thomas the Seannachie, from his chair by the chimney corner, had been watching him closely. The man's eyes, glittering pale blue in the firelight, seemed to see clear through the casing of skull and hair to the darkest thought.

They sat, king and storyteller, transfixed, bound to each other for seconds, sharing fear and pain. And then gradually, as if from far off, the laughter and voices of the others washed back around them, breaking the bridge.

'Music, Seannachie, and a tale to round the day.'

Thomas nodded, stooped, and lifting a small harp began to play. The group around the table fell silent as he crooned softly in a voice of wine and honey, an old ballad of love and courage, faith and trust.

Enchantment lay in every word, turning each one's thoughts inward to his dearest dreams.

The old duke grunted softly, remembering

again his young wife, long since dead. He saw
her face, round and freckled as a hen's egg, and
the unruly copper curls. Young Wat had his
father's strong features but his mother's
colouring and green eyes. Those eyes that were
now gazing moonstruck at Marion Elliot.

The old duke smiled fondly. They were fair daft
about each other those two, despite the fact that
all their early years had been spent in fighting like
farmyard cats. Wat and Allan Elliot were the same
age, inseparable as boys, and wee Marion,
devoted to her brother, had tagged along
everywhere behind them, in and out of their
troubles, creating plenty of her own. There was
the time when Wat and Allan had tied her pigtails
together round a pillar in church. What a
screeching she had set up when she found she
couldn't move. They were all three skelped
soundly for that escapade! Then there was the
day when the boys left Marion at home to go
swimming. She followed them, found their
clothes, and filled the boots with cold porridge.
He laughed aloud again at the memory.

And now, here they were at last, as everyone
had always known they should be, longing for
the day when they would finally be married.

No bad thing either, thought the shrewd
old duke, seeing in his mind's eye the rich
Elliot fields lying snug alongside Wat's estate of
Branxholm. When the old ones were gone it

27

would strengthen the boy's position to have Allan Elliot standing as a brother by his side.

The last notes of the Seannachie's song died away. In the golden firelight a mood of sleepiness settled on the company. A log cracked in the grate. The duke's favourite hound crunched softly on a bone under the table. The king sighed, behind his chair the pageboy crouched, sound asleep, his back against the heavy tapestry wall hanging. Marion nestled against Wat's shoulder, stifling a yawn. He lifted a lock of her long silky brown hair on his fingertip and rubbed it against his cheek, longing for the moment to last, if not for ever, then at least a little longer.

'One more story, old friend,' he begged. 'We would have one more tale to send us peaceful to bed.'

'A ghost story,' demanded Allan. 'Something to chill the blood.'

'Aye, that would take my fancy too,' said the king, loathe to leave the company for a lonely bed.

'Very well, my lord, so be it.'

The Seannachie laid down his harp, took a deep breath as if to begin, then stopped. He sat as if listening to a call unheard by the others, then rose slowly from the chair before the fire. His shadow spreading over them all filled the room.

Into the hush there came the stamp of heavy boots, the clang of iron against stone on the spiral staircase.

Each man around the king sat up suddenly, sober and alert, hands reaching for sword or dagger. Wat was instantly on his feet facing the door, pushing Marion behind him.

'A tale there will be, my lords,' whispered Thomas the Seannachie in a chilling voice. 'But not of my telling. One comes to unfold it even now.'

Outside the door the voice of Andrew, Wat's most trusted servant, could be heard raised in fury.

The latch on the heavy door lifted with a crash, it swung slowly open on creaking hinges. In the sharp draught the smoking candles flickered. The duke's hound abandoned his bone and crept, snarling, beneath his master's chair.

Into the charmed ring of light stepped the thin, elegant, black-clad figure of the king's cousin, Ranulf de Soulis. He pulled off his black gauntlets, tossed them on the table and stood smiling, his widespread hands empty.

For a split second they sat around the table as if turned to stone, then relief washed over them. The duke rose to greet this uninvited guest. Soulis, disregarding him, stepped forward with a low bow towards the king.

'Sire, cousin Robert de Bruce, I trust I find you well?'

Tension around the table eased. The duke's

hound settled again to his bone. Swords slid silently into sheaths.

'Indeed, my Lord Soulis,' said the king. 'Although I come amongst you unheralded, as a plain man, I find that welcome awaits me wherever I turn. News of my presence, it would seem, goes before me.'

'Good news, they say, Sire, travels fast.'

Moving round the table, black and silent as a shadow, Soulis lifted an apple, spun it by some sleight-of-hand on long fingers, then bit hard into the crisp flesh.

'Wine for Lord Soulis, make haste there, boy!' Wat clapped his hands.

The sleepy page staggered to his feet to fill another goblet. Soulis stood waiting as the boy approached, carefully offering the wine at arm's length. He caught the goblet and the shaking hand in his own. The boy pulled back, and then stopped, held in the tightly gripping fingertips.

There was panic in his eyes as he faced Soulis. He too had heard the rumours from the other servants, and had seen a field of corn said to have been blighted because his lordship coveted the land on which it grew. In the market place at Hawick he had heard tales of cattle dying, men and women falling sick under the spell of that evil touch. Choking back terror, he tried again to pull free.

'Let the child go, my lord!' Wat moved towards

them. Soulis, laughing, released the boy's hand suddenly. The wine jerked in the goblet, splashing the tunics of both. Laughter died in his face as Soulis lifted a hand to strike out.

'My lord!' The king's voice rang out, stern and commanding. But the blow never fell. Quick as a flash, Marion Elliot stepped between Soulis and the page.

'It is long since time this boy was in bed, and you, my lord, would surely find better sport amongst your equals.'

Stopped in his tracks, Soulis glared at the girl who had dared to cross him. Little bigger than a child herself, Marion glared back, defying the cold black eyes. Soulis threw back his head and laughed.

'But my dear lady, here I *have* no equal. I count myself as nothing before my king.' He bowed low in the direction of Robert. 'And as a mere soldier, cannot compare my humble person with these worthy and noble – farmers – amongst whom you chose to dine.'

'You go too far, my lord!' hissed Wat, drawing Marion aside.

'But in jest, merely in jest, Master Scott,' said Soulis lightly. He turned to study Marion as the light by the table fell full on her, glowing on the long shining auburn hair, the creamy skin and the simple blue woollen gown.

'And this, I take it, is your future bride? Beauty

31

and spirit both? Who would have thought it possible? You must allow me the privilege of entertaining you at Hermitage.' His words were addressed to Marion only. 'Amongst my poor treasures none would shine more brightly.'

Marion shivered and moved closer to Wat. Her hand slipped into his.

'You are cold perhaps, my lady?' whispered Soulis gently.

'No, my lord,' Marion answered loud and firm. 'But tired. I fear I must bid you good night and withdraw.'

'Fear?' breathed Soulis. 'Why do you fear? You have strength, Mistress Elliot, and courage – qualities a man would value.' He glanced at Wat, a sneering smile curling his lips. 'A *man*, Mistress Elliot. You waste them on this boy.'

Wat, his temper finally pushed to the limit, elbowed Marion aside and faced Soulis, dagger in hand.

'Stop him! The daft laddie's drunk!' The old duke was on his feet at the same instant.

'Enough,' roared the king, spurred into action at last. 'This fooling must cease!'

'Indeed, Sire,' said Soulis smoothly, 'it is but child's play.'

He gazed slowly round the table at each man there, his black eyes commanding their attention, then turned and raised his hand. Staring straight into Wat's furious face he pushed hard with open palm against the glittering point of the dagger.

Wat stood, rigid. Willing all his strength into his arm, he pushed back. The others watched in horror as the blade, powerless against that slight narrow hand with the delicate musician's fingers, bent back and upwards.

With a sudden sweeping snatch, Soulis seized the knife in his bare fingers and tore it from Wat's grasp.

'Mere child's play!' he laughed, sending it spinning with a clatter into the dead ashes of the hearth. He held up his hand, palm outward, in a gesture of mocking peace, and Wat, his heart pounding, sickness rising in his throat, stared in open disbelief. The white skin was perfect, unmarked as any fine lady's.

Marion stepped back softly into the shadows, gathering her skirts around her.

'Mistress Elliot,' whispered Soulis, his blazing eyes holding Wat's irresistibly. Shaking, she turned to the king who stood helpless in rage . . .

'Sire.' Dropping a curtsey she moved gingerly past Soulis, as if even to touch him with the hem of her dress would spread the contamination of his presence. He watched her every step of the way.

'Mistress Elliot,' his soft voice carried clear across the deathly hush. In the darkness by the door she hesitated and turned to face him.

He stood smiling, hand on heart, in a playful

33

lovesick gesture. In the candlelight strange shadows danced across the thin, handsome face.

'Good night – but not goodbye. We will meet again, you and I. Sleep well.'

A log fell in the fire, sending a shower of sparks up the chimney. Thomas the Seannachie, gazing into the glowing embers, shook his head, reading there the tale of times yet to be.

# Three

## 'I have need of you, little brother'

High above the bleak moonlit wilderness of Liddesdale and the windswept peaks of Black Edge, an owl swooped, hung silver and ghost-like against the stars, and dived deadly as an avenging angel. Along the banks of the Liddel Water, terrified creatures huddled together in holes and burrows, tiny pockets of warmth and life in the cold river mist.

The owl lifted, with the wind whistling an eerie note through his pinion feathers, and struck out for the rich hunting grounds where the Liddel and Hermitage Waters met, beneath the massive windowless walls of the castle of Lord Soulis, master of all the Border lands around.

The castle lay quiet. Cooks and serving boys snored in warm dirty corners of the smoke-blackened greasy kitchen. Ostlers nestled in the sweet-smelling straw of the stables. Here and there a horse whinnied softly in his stall, a hound yelped, twitching uneasily in troubled dreams.

Around an iron brazier in the tiny enclosed

35

courtyard, those few men left standing guard huddled closer together.

'A fine night.'

'Aye, peaceful for once.' Somewhere in the castle a woman's voice yelped, half in fun, followed by a man's smothered laugh.

'Right enough, when the de'il's away . . .'

They whispered amongst themselves, crouched within the ring of firelight as if afraid to venture into the blackness beyond, or fearful of some unseen listener lurking in the shadows. They knew that Soulis had left for Branxholm hours before, alone and riding in a fury. But still the fear that hung about him like the river mist lingered on. The whispered words of his men were few and terse, guarding their deepest thoughts.

Above them in a tiny tower room, Gibbie lay alone on a thin heather-stuffed mattress. Moonlight from the one window slit lanced across the damp stone floor, picking out the rough blanket on the bed, the boy's thin white face and his eyes, shining black and brilliant and wide open.

His skin was cold to the touch, his light breath scarcely stirring the rough shirt in which he slept. He lay like a figure carved in stone, frozen and lifeless.

Turmoil reigned, though, in the darkness behind his eyes. Ignoring hunger and pain, he clutched to himself the few hours of freedom from the constant tormenting presence of Soulis.

A suffocating wave of loathing swept over him at the thought of the man, flooding his mind and twisting his body so that his fist clenched of its own accord tightly round the pendant.

Aware at last of the pain, Gibbie opened his cramped fingers. In the moonlight he could see that the tarnished metal had cut the skin. He traced again the old familiar heraldic figures, hearing his mother's voice.

'Hold fast to it, laddie. It is yours by right – the birth-gift of your most noble father – may he rot in hell!'

His most noble father! From his earliest days Gibbie had always known himself different from the other children. He and his mother lived in a hovel on the edge of the wood, driven out of the village for some crime committed before his birth. They would have burned her for a witch, but feared her friendship with the lord who came and went in the night.

Gibbie was teased and bullied by the village children. Finally learning to hit back in a rage with fists and curses, he had earned a grudging respect for his violent temper and was gradually left in peace.

Tongues still wagged behind their backs, but in whispers.

'No better than she should be.'

'That lad's bound to come to a bad end, d'you

mind the old laird?'

'Clacking tongues. They've little else in their heads to concern them,' sneered Gibbie's mother.

They ignored the talk and drew further and further apart from the villagers, keeping to themselves in the ramshackle hut where Gibbie's mother, recalling some long-lost past of which she never spoke, taught her son to read and write.

Whatever that past had been, Gibbie's father, the old Lord Soulis, despised her for it. At the same time though, consumed with pride, he insisted that his son should know his lineage and wear the crest of Soulis. Her belief, clung to throughout the long years of hardship, had always been that one day Gibbie would inherit his rightful position and so must be prepared for it. She had hung the pendant about his neck and kept alive, in fostering his pride and arrogance, the image of the man who had left her unmarried and with a child, to face the world alone.

Gibbie had never seen his father. Indeed, while his mother kept his memory alive, she seemed to live in constant fear that the man would one day return, perhaps to claim his son. She waited only for his death so that Gibbie might lay claim one day to his rightful share of a great inheritance.

The chance came at last in his thirteenth year. In the depths of a vicious winter his mother lay sick, wasted by years of poverty. It had been a bad year with early autumn rains destroying what little harvest there was. Plague, fever and rats followed close on the heels of the hunger that winter. Gibbie tramped about the countryside, begging for work, hoarding or stealing scraps of food to take back to the hut. It was in the frozen mists of a black winter night, lurking in an inn yard, that he had overheard men talking of the death of the old lord, his father.

He raced back to his mother with the news. Again and again she made him repeat the words. She dragged herself from the bed, eyes bright with fever and snatched at the pendant around his neck.

'So the old fiend's dead at last,' she crowed. 'The De'il has come for his own!' Gibbie fell back, astonished at the strength in the dried claw-like hands, revolted by the sores on the rotting skin, and her breath reeking of sickness.

'Your half-brother is the man of power now, Gibbie,' she breathed hoarsely, clinging to him. 'We must take this pendant to him. He cannot deny it. Blood must call out to blood.'

Gibbie stirred uneasily on his narrow bed as he remembered how that half-brother had welcomed them.

Ranulf de Soulis, son of his own father, newly created Lord of Liddesdale, had his men drag them before him for sport. They had been kicked and spat on. His mother, racked with pain and fever, was thrown at the feet of his lordship, while Gibbie was held helpless and watching.

'Impertinent scum!' Soulis grabbed her by the throat and hauled her gasping to her knees. His voice, hardly raised above a murmur, was cold as ice. 'You would drag this . . . trash . . . into my home and pass him off as my half-brother? How shall I repay you for this kindness?'

His gloved fist lashed out and sent her sprawling across the floor.

'You presume on my hospitality, madam?' His laugh was echoed by his men. 'Then fetch them to my dungeon!' he snarled and the laugh died in their throats.

Gibbie struggled uselessly as they stepped forward to drag his mother from the hall. With a strength born of desperation she slipped from their grasp and fell clutching at the feet of Soulis.

'See that?' she screamed. 'You would deny your own blood – your own damned blood!'

She fell back, her lifeless fingers still pointing to where Gibbie struggled. His torn shirt had fallen open revealing the pendant. With two steps Soulis was in front of him.

'How came you by this?'

'She – gave it me . . .' Gibbie's choking voice was hardly coherent through his tears. 'She said it was the birth-gift of my father.'

'Liar! Stolen, not given. I will have the truth,

though I have to drag it from this witch by torture.'

But Gibbie's mother was beyond truth or torture, and in death Gibbie saw on her lips the first smile he could remember in many a long year.

Soulis turned and stared at Gibbie, long and hard. The men holding him loosed their grip and stepped back watching their master closely. They were terrified of him, Gibbie realised, even more afraid than he had been. He stared back into those fathomless black eyes defiantly. They were almost a mirror image of his own.

'You wish to claim your rights, peasant? Then you shall have them. You shall eat of my food and drink of my wine, and may even sleep under my roof. You would claim brotherhood with me and your birthright as a Soulis? Then you shall have it my fine lad. Whether you will or not – you shall have it.'

For the first time, listening to that soft whisper, Gibbie felt real chilling fear. Soulis read it in his eyes and laughed.

'But remember, Gilbert de Soulis, you have chosen of your own free will, and must accept the consequences. If ever you try to leave here I will have you hunted down to be strangled on the gallows as a thief!'

'But it is mine by right . . . ,' gasped Gibbie. But Soulis had gone, snapping orders to his men to remove the body of Gibbie's mother and have

41

her buried on the moor.

So for half a year Gibbie had remained through winter, spring and summer in the Castle of Hermitage at the whim and fancy of Soulis, learning piece by piece the secrets of his brother's power, and finding himself dragged ever deeper into that evil web. He watched and listened, biding his time against the day when he might use that power to his own ends.

A shout and clatter of arms from the courtyard dragged him back from his thoughts. He rolled wearily from the bed and peered down on to the dusty moonlit road.

The beat of hooves, a horse approaching fast, careering through the dark at breakneck speed, broke the silence. No ordinary man in his right mind would ride the forest paths at dead of night in that way. But this, thought Gibbie, was no ordinary man, and who knew where his mind lay?

The hoofbeats thundered closer, clattering beneath him, and Gibbie watched as Soulis dragged his horse, flecked with foam, to a furious halt by the gateway. Torches flickered, shouts rang out and the castle sprang into life.

'Gibbie!' Even in his high chamber Gibbie could feel the rage in that voice. His lordship had been thwarted in some desire no doubt, stung by some insult, imagined or otherwise. Gibbie hauled on his boots and tunic, and staggered down the twisting stone staircase to come face to face with his terrifying half-brother, who stood framed in the arched doorway, an unholy moonlit halo framing his dark head.

Soulis reached out a hand. Gibbie stepped back smartly, expecting a blow which never fell.

'Gibbie,' suddenly gentle and persuasive, Soulis was at his most dangerous. 'There is work for you tonight. I have need of you, little brother.'

Gibbie's heart skipped a beat, then thumped choking in his throat. At one and the same time terror and excitement filled him. Soulis slipped an arm round the boy's thin shoulders and led him across the courtyard to a flight of steps that led down to a low door. Turning, he spoke to his men:

'Guard well, my friends, guard well. But let it be known that if any man among you should speak of what he may see or hear this night, he will have neither eyes to see nor tongue to speak again.'

'My lord.' They pulled their cloaks around them as if to contain their fear and turned away from their master, who stood with Gibbie in the flickering torchlight by the steps. It was plain then for all to see that the two faces were linked by the blood of their father.

'Lock the gates!' called Soulis. 'And let no man

come or go until daybreak. Come, Gibbie, you and I this night shall prepare to meet our true master.'

His arm lay easy across Gibbie's shoulder, but the fingertips, gripping like an eagle's talons through shirt and tunic, bruised the bone beneath as he led the boy down the stairs and through the low doorway into the foul and stinking dungeons of Hermitage . . .

# Four

## Who sups with the devil

In the low vaulted stone ante-chamber, the only light came from their smoking torch. The flame flickered, dancing in the draught as Soulis kicked the door shut with a crash that echoed through and through that terrible place.

'Now, Gibbie, we are alone for the moment, you and I.' His face was alight with an unholy joy. Lifting the torch high he set off along the twisting damp passageway, dragging Gibbie with him.

Deeper and deeper they went, through cramped narrow tunnels of roughly cut stone, down worn stairways where rats scuttled ahead of them, their eyes gleaming like jewels in the blackness. The light fell briefly on rot and mould, on crumbling wood and rusting chains, on a rickle of bones twisted and huddled in a corner, and passed on quickly as if afraid to reveal too much.

Gibbie clenched his teeth on sickness. However

45

often he retraced these steps his body still revolted at the stench.

They came at last to the deepest level, to a heavy iron door. Cut into the damp slime-covered stone above the lintel were strange signs and markings, their meaning clear for all to read

Our Lord's crucifix, defaced and inverted, was surrounded by other crosses, their arms broken and twisted. On either side was carved the crest of Soulis, that same heraldic badge that had hung around Gibbie's neck since birth.

Gibbie took a deep breath, and held his teeth clenched shut as Soulis unbolted the last door. After the clinging damp of the dungeon they were suddenly engulfed in a wave of stifling, foetid warmth.

He followed Soulis as if in a trance.

The room was small. The curving roof was supported on massive stone pillars like huge fossilised tree trunks. Soulis stepped silently across the dry earthen floor.

'Take care,' whispered Gibbie. 'Oh, take care . . .'

But Soulis, beyond hearing, approached the only object in the room, a huge metal-bound chest on which sat an old battered pewter jug. Raising his arms, he spread his long fine hands in welcome.

'Spirit, I come.'

'Come . . . come . . .' echoed the walls.

'Spirit, I come.'

Gibbie threw his hands over his ears as the echoes, fading into each other, set up a deep resonant hum that grew in strength as if a thousand insects filled the air.

'Spirit, I come!' called Soulis for the third time, and the very stones cried back in greeting.

'Now, Gibbie, now!' He dragged the boy forward pushing the jug into his hands.

Gibbie held it before him at arm's length, as if the metal burned, shaking with fear and anticipation.

Soulis took from his pouch a small leather bottle, opened it and held it high between them so that a steady stream of liquid, dark and glistening, poured into the jug. The smell of fresh blood filled their nostrils. Across their outstretched hands, Gibbie's eyes met those of Soulis.

'Tears, Gibbie?'

He shook the bottle and the last dark drops fell from the lip.

'It is but one mouth less for the starving fools to feed. I do a favour to these peasants.'

He unsheathed his dagger, and dipping it in the blood, drew with the blade a curious twisting pattern on the dusty floor before the chest. He knelt, the blade gleaming in his hands, and his commanding voice rang out.

'Now, pour, Gibbie! From a child of the House

of Soulis, the gift is potent indeed.'

Torn between fascination and horror, Gibbie hesitated. Beside him the dagger flashed. Before him the iron-bound chest seemed to pulsate with his thumping heart. Hardly aware of what he was doing, he stepped forward holding the jug high.

'Come, Spirit, come,' breathed Soulis and the blood ran in a steady trickle to fall in the centre of the strange whirling pattern in the sand. The sound of the quiet trickle grew louder, filling the ears, filling the head, filling the senses as if a great river flowed about them. The smell of blood came thick and choking.

With his eardrums bursting, his face burning, Gibbie dropped the jug and staggered back until his hands, meeting the dry roughness of the stone, stopped him. He shrank as if desperate to make himself invisible and half-crawled from the room.

Behind him, a voice, neither man nor woman, child nor ancient, whispered as if from the tomb.

'What now would you have of me? What want ye, Soulis?'

'Power, Lord,' whispered Soulis. 'I would be king. It is my right – my due.'

'I gave to thee that which thou asked already. The gift of strength that each man's weapon might fall useless against thy body. Is not that enough?'

'Indeed, Great Lord. But what is strength without power? Give me the crown, that none may challenge it and I alone may hold it safe against our enemies.'

'There is a king, Soulis, to whom you have sworn fealty.'

'But he is weak and sickly. Like to die.'

'Then wait you, my lord, wait you.' The voice faded hoarsely. Soulis leapt to his feet, the jug clanging against the chest.

'No! Wait *you*, Spirit. I pay your price. I demand your favours.'

'Then this I will tell you, Soulis. The time will come when all men kneel before you.'

'When, Spirit, when.'

'Soon enough, Soulis. The time will come . . . when it will come.'

'Then grant me now that which I desire, Spirit. It may be that I must wait for the crown, but I would have young Branxholm's bride to be my queen. Grant me that, Dark Spirit!' Lifting the jug high he let the blood spill, splashing the chest and his swirling cloak.

'This wish I may grant, foolish mortal.'

'Mortal . . . mortal . . . ,' echoed the vault in mocking whispers.

'Tomorrow eve young Branxholm's bride shall sit within thy walls.'

'Oh, Gracious Spirit . . .'

'But hear this that I tell thee. Invoke me not for

seven years more, nor open the door of this vault. Soulis, thou hast already demanded more than thy due.'

'Master, thy will be done . . .'

'Go now, follow thy chosen path. But heed you, Soulis, heed you my last warning. Beware the coming wood . . . the coming wood . . .'

Gibbie, crouching by the door, buried his head in his arms, shaking with terror.

'Beware the coming wood!'

The voice faded to a dying note which lingered, slowly growing to a great gale howling through the dungeon, snatching at their clothes, battering the breath from their lungs.

Hours later, coming to his senses, Gibbie stumbled back into the room. Soulis crouched by the chest, his eyes glazed, drugged by the stifling deadly air.

The empty jug lay on an earthen floor scoured clean and dry, unmarked by blood or knife-blade.

Soulis lifted the jug and carefully placed it on the chest. Then reaching out a hand to Gibbie, came slowly to his feet. Drained of all feeling, they staggered from the room, each avoiding the other's eyes.

The torch in the bracket by the door burnt low to a guttering flicker, scarcely illuminating the symbols carved above them.

Without a word spoken, the two brothers made their way back up through the foul passageways of the dungeon to the bleak courtyard and the cold, half-light of dawn.

## Five

### Frost on a summer morning

The king reined in his horse and turned back in the saddle for a last longing look at the soft farmland and rich forests of the wide Border country. Behind him lay the precious peace of the few stolen days spent hunting in the company of trusted friends. Ahead of him lay the cares of Council and State, roosting like carrion crows above the windswept battlements of his draughty fortress by the sea at Ayr.

At his back rode Wat Scott and his father. That at least gave the king comfort. The duke had fought alongside him when he himself was Wat's age, and the crown an impossible dream. Now it was his, and would remain his with the support of the duke and his men. But behind the duke, thought King Robert with satisfaction, came Wat, young, strong, already proving himself a good man in a fight and an even better one at the Council table.

The old duke was a man of action, none could

dispute that, but inclined to rage and storm over the interminable discussions and compromises necessary to keep the peace around the throne. Wat, though, was different. He had his father's courage, but he knew too how to bide his time. Normally slow to anger, he had the gift of patience and a persuasive, quiet charm that led men to follow him. All the more reason then, the king realised, to keep Wat at his side in a position of influence and to let it be seen that he had the king's love and trust.

All the more reason too, and the thought nagged at him like a toothache, to fear his outburst against Soulis.

Robert knew that there would one day come a final battle between these two, and that he must be seen to support one or the other. But which?

Soulis was strong and powerful with a rightful claim to the throne. He was of old Norman stock, still after several generations seen as foreigners, loathed and feared by all who knew him. Not for the first time Robert sent a quiet thanks to his father who had married into the old Celtic royal line.

Wat, on the other hand, was heir to a long line of fighters, farmers and Border reivers. He belonged to the green hills as they did to him. He was of the people, and to his cause they would flock in an army that might threaten the throne itself.

The king could affort to lose the support of neither man, and so Soulis had returned unchecked to Hermitage, and Wat rode with him to Ayr, a trusted member of the Council.

'Troubled thoughts, Sire, make poor company on the road.'

The Seannachie had ridden silently up beside the king, who had commanded his presence on the journey. Robert shook his head, and the man fell back again, sensing the king's need to be alone with his thoughts.

Thomas the Seannachie had come at his command right enough. The duke had suggested that a far-fetched tale or saga of some long-forgotten battle might pass the weary journey and lighten the long evenings at Ayr. The storyteller, though, had seemed reluctant to leave Branxholm.

Who could blame him, thought Robert, admiring the glowing smile and laughing eyes of Marion Elliot. She rode with Wat on one side and her brother Allan on the other, surrounded by their friends. Even in all that young and happy company she shone like a jewel. The Seannachie, in a fine flow of rich wine and poetry had named her the Bonniest Rose in All the Border, and that was certainly how she seemed in the morning sunlight. Fresh as the dew, a wild rose, small and pink in a cloud of soft green velvet, but with that thorny tongue. The laughter rose and fell around her as she teased Wat. These two would have a lively marriage, of that there was no doubt.

Robert watched the young people with a twinge of envy. They carried with them an air of lightness and festival as they joked and sang amongst themselves.

'Daft young limmers!' grunted the duke, plodding happily along, the sun at his back, his eyes on a future held safe by a strong young son and grandchildren yet to be.

Robert envied him, remembering his own son, whose birthright must be jealously guarded in his years of weakness by this chain of Border lords. Scott, Douglas, Soulis . . .

Soulis . . . Soulis. The name tolled like a plague bell in his mind.

He saw again in his mind's eye the scene at Branxholm. Soulis daring in his insolence to challenge the king's authority. And yet what had he said? The challenge lay not in the man's words, but in his very presence. Robert knew full well that there were those among his councillors who would have Soulis secretly murdered, but there had been enough of that in the bad times. Divided and squabbling amongst themselves his lords would leave a pathway to the throne wide open to the enemy. Together they must build a wall to hold the kingdom safe from harm. The king dared not be seen to break that wall, so Soulis – God help him – must be protected.

And yet . . . and yet. There was that incident with Wat. The flesh that defied the iron blade. Robert shook his head, still muzzy from the smoke and wine of the previous night, and tried again to recall clearly the image. What they had seen was not possible, some trickery perhaps. Soulis was known for it.

It could not have been. Yet he had seen what he had seen.

His eyes caught those of the Seannachie. Had he seen what he had seen? The thought passed between them. The Seannachie nodded slowly.

It was as if a frost had settled on that summer morning.

Their mood was broken by a shout as the others came jingling up the path towards the crossroads where they must part company.

Saying her goodbyes to Wat, Marion kept her tears in check.

'God go with you, my love. The days will seem endless without you.'

'Soon, Wat, soon. We must have patience.'

'I have no patience when I'm away from you, Marion, nor ever will again.'

They stood apart from the others, longing to say so much, yet at a loss for words.

'I'll come with you, Wat. Call me your pageboy – I'll wear one of Allen's tunics, it wouldn't be the first time! Or wrap me in your baggage and I'll hide in your quarters, even your father'll never know.'

'Hide! You! You'd never be able to stay quiet long enough. They'd hear you talking to the bedpost.' They laughed and fell silent again.

'I would to God I could go with you, Wat.'

'I know. As long as we're apart I am afraid for you.'

This was a new Wat, suddenly serious, troubled and uncertain.

'Afraid of what? I would as soon lose my life as leave you?'

'I know, lass, I know.' He paused. 'But we must leave – and Soulis stays here.'

'Och, Wat! Soulis is jealous. Filled with hate, but we have love you and I, and where there is love and hate, love is aye the stronger. The priest says so.'

'Wat! Come on, lad, we're leaving!' They kissed a last sad-sweet farewell. Then suddenly, turning to leave he stopped, reached into his jerkin and took from around his neck the leather thong on which he wore the little wooden cross his mother had given him.

'Pray God keep you safe, Marion. Pray God.' He placed the cross round her neck, then turning to Allan grasped him by the shoulders.

'Please, I beg you,' he said, and the laughter died in Allan's eyes before his look. 'Guard her safe for me. Cherish her as I would until my return.'

57

'I will, Wat. I promise you I will.'

He had made his final farewells then and followed the others on the road to Ayr, quickly and without looking back.

Marion wept to see him go, but Allan and the others rallied to cheer her on the road home.

'A coronet for the bride!' sang her friend and bridesmaid-to-be, Annie Graham, and they laughed and crowned her with a garland of buttercups, daisies and sweet-smelling honeysuckle.

Gradually her heart lifted and she joined with the others racing side by side across the flat meadows by the river bank. They chased panting after Allan's hound as it raised a rabbit on a sunlight hillside, and laughed to see it leap for cover down a burrow, leaving the dog scraping, puzzled at the sandy earth, tail wagging furiously.

They came at last to rest in the cool shade of a sunlit clearing in the wood by the Teviot Water and sprawled laughing in the long grass.

'The feast, slaves,' demanded Allan clapping his hands. 'Spread me your sweetmeats. Fetch me your dainties.' With a flourish he produced a flask of wine. From other pouches and saddlebags came bread and cheese and fruit. A cloak was thrown on the grass and a meal soon spread before them.

The long afternoon wore on in a haze of golden

sunlight. They talked and sang and guddled for fish in the burn. Allan set off into the wood with Annie to search for sweet-smelling herbs for her mother's larder.

Marion, singing softly to herself, wandered among the trees, her mind flying free with the white puffy clouds, or with Wat on the dusty road to Ayr.

A harsh croak cut through the dreamy tangle of thought. Opening her eyes wide she found herself in a dark and overgrown place where the trees clustered together blotting out the sun. A rough moss-grown cliff face rose before her. Water dripped, glistening, from the jagged rock and hung like crystal beads from each tiny stem and flower. At the foot of the cliff was a pool, deep and dark, perfectly round and edged with roughly cut stones as if some hand, many years since, had created a well.

A pert black and white magpie perched gaudily on the low stone wall, watching her with cunning eyes. The bird seemed quite fearless. He opened his beak and again the harsh mocking cry rang off the cliff face, the tone almost questioning.

Marion stepped forward carefully.

'Whose wee bird are you then? Have you a master?'

One year the travelling fair had come to Hawick bringing with them clowns and acrobats and a strange bird that spoke to them almost as if he were a man enchanted. This bird had the same air of assurance, and lack of fear. He hopped from one leg to the other, moving back restlessly.

'Come, birdie, come. I'll not hurt ye. Come to me, come to me.'

Suddenly it seemed to her as if the one thought in her head was that she must have the bird. Cautiously she crept across the lush green moss, her fingers outstretched, her voice croodling softly like a mother to her child.

'Come, birdie, come. I'll take good care of ye. I want you for my own.'

The bird side-stepped delicately round the rim of the well by the still dark water, where ferns and reeds lightly tipped their reflections.

Marion froze in mid-step. Her heart stopped with a thump. The world seemed to shift about her crazily. The bird's eye, more knowing than ever, and colder than the furthest star, blinked once. He rose flapping noisily from the stones and fled to the tree tops, leaving his mocking call to echo round the woods.

The ruffled water settled again to a clear mirror reflecting ferns, flowers and trees, and nothing else. There had been nothing else.

The bird, so bright, so real, had cast no image on the dark water.

A quiet laugh brought Marion, gasping, to her senses. She spun round and came face to face with the Lord of Liddesdale, Ranulf de Soulis.

'Ah, my wayward pet.' He stepped softly through the grass, smiling sweetly.

'My lord?'

'My lady.' He bowed extravagantly, with a flutter of his long fine fingers. 'It would seem you found my wayward pet – my other self – poor pied pathetic creature. Before him the silly songbirds flee in terror.'

He came towards her, his black eyes sparkling. She swallowed, her voice choking in her throat. From far off through the trees came faintly the sound of Allan and her friends calling her name.

'Marion! Marion!'

'Marion,' whispered Soulis, almost as if tasting the word.

'Marion! Where are you? We must go back now.'

Speech froze on her lips. Her eyes held by his, she shook her head. He smiled and reaching forward gently took her by the wrist.

'No – no . . .' she whispered, feeling his fingertips a cold ring of imprisoning iron. It was as if her legs had lost the strength to resist. He drew her slowly back towards the trees where his horse stood tied. And all the while his voice murmured in her ear.

'Come hell, come heaven, I will have you, Marion Elliot, for my own. And you are promised to me.'

'I am promised to Wat Scott, as well you know.'

Slowly, slowly he led her back. No power on earth could have resisted his. The very trees would topple to his command.

'My lord, my lord! I beg you.'

Her voice was lost in the rustle of the wind-tossed leaves, and still he drew her on.

'Marion! Marion!' If she could only shout they must hear her. She turned back, waving a helpless hand in their direction.

'Poor stupid fools! What want you with the likes of them, Marion? You may – you must – have me, and all that I can give you.' His words were gentle, almost pleading.

Marion, blinded with tears, could only shake her head.

'Wat . . . Wat . . .' she wept. A note of steel entered his voice as Soulis dragged her the last few steps to his horse.

'You could not dream what I can give you, Marion, what is within my power to give. For you the wonders of the world shall be spread at my command. It is beyond the wit of little minds to comprehend.'

'No, my lord. I want none of it.'

'I *will* show you, and you *must* come to me . . .'

They were close now, crashing through the bracken. Allen's voice rang through the wood.

'Marion . . . Marion . . . Marion . . .'

Soulis swung into the saddle, dragging her kicking and struggling before him. Her fists beat helplessly against him.

He snatched up the reins and, booting the horse, galloped off into the darkness of the trees. Fighting against him Marion suddenly found herself clutching the little childhood crucifix Wat had put round her neck.

She gripped it tightly, and on a sudden Wat's warmth and love seemed to rush through her hand, her arm, and into her whole body, unfreezing the fear that gripped her. Unlocking the silent voice.

'Help me!' she screamed, 'Allan – help me!'

Soulis swore and tried to pull her hand from the cross, but again, fighting for breath she found her voice.

'Soulis . . . Soulis . . . Soulis . . .' as if screaming some terrible curse, and the word faded with their dying hoofbeats.

# Six

## The House of Soulis

She sat hunched on the high bed. The little room was dark and airless, cold even in the heat of summer. The walls hung with heavy tapestries, once rich, now smelling of decay.

From the courtyard Marion could hear the constant coming and going of men arming themselves, the clang of blacksmith's hammer on iron, the grate of sharpening stone on blade. The preparations for killing.

Cutting across the noise, clear and firm, came the voice of Soulis. She slid from the bed and dragged a low stool, the only other piece of furniture in the room, to the tiny window. The bolt on the solid shutter was stiff and rusted, but gave at last. Straining to see, but not be seen, she pulled back the shutter and peered down.

In the dark well of the tiny enclosed yard the brazier burned brightly. Firelight gleamed on moss-covered paving stones that saw no sun. Shadows, like misshapen giants, danced on the walls as the men went about their work. Here there was no talk or laughter, as she heard at Branxholm or amongst her father's people. These men seemed sullen and subdued. They stopped only to exchange an order in low tones. Those who had to address Soulis did so as if approaching some savage and unpredictable beast.

He stood in the centre, directing operations, snapping orders in a low crisp voice, seeming calm and ordered in the bustle. And yet, even from high above, Marion could sense the hatred and fury surrounding him, and the anger tightly controlled in his voice. His was the calm of the eye of the storm.

None dared stand against him, that way lay death. But for all that, Marion could feel that a different mood had crept in, growing through that long day. She could feel the sullen discontent. They watched him carefully enough and with hate-filled eyes. Where before they had followed him without question, they now seemed to shun him as the pack does a lone mad beast.

Soulis saw their fear, and feeding on it he relished it, but he saw too their hatred and contempt, more obvious since the woman had come, more open that it had ever been. The anger rose in his throat.

Throughout his life Soulis had lived with fear. Growing in the shadow of a father whose evil he had learned early, dragged as a child into the secret ways of witchcraft, he saw that the power of the House of Soulis lay in fear. He who would rule must wield that power to his own end. He had been taught well and viciously, that no gentleness, no love, must ever weaken his strength. He lived and prospered, protected by the evil that for generations had held his family in thrall.

It was the creed of the House of Soulis that no humanity must touch his soul. There was no power in hell or on earth stronger than hate, and all men cringed before it – even the king.

But not Marion Elliot. She had stood before him, that child-woman and openly defied him. He was accustomed to see men turn to challenge him, their faces a false mask of courage betrayed by the fear in their eyes.

But not Marion Elliot. Confident in the rightness of her cause, she had shown only anger, her eyes blazing with honest rage. For the first time, a woman had stood before him challenging and aggressive, and he had felt a ridiculous longing, not to hurt, but to capture her, to have that spirit stand not against, but alongside him.

Since that time the obsession had grown in his mind. Wherever he turned he saw Marion Elliot's furious face, her blazing defiance, her soft curling brown hair. The feeling unnerved and infuriated him.

Consumed by fury he lashed out with his whip against the cobbles, and his men, seeing unreasoning rage flash in the diamond-bright eyes, shrank like rats into the shadows, each hoping to escape his notice.

Soulis swept from the courtyard and stormed up the twisting staircase to his room.

'Gibbie! Gibbie! I would have wine. NOW!'

Gibbie, watching him closely, had already anticipated that demand. The wine stood waiting in his chamber.

Soulis threw himself into the huge black oak chair carved for his grandfather. A throne for a king who never was. He poured glass after glass, drinking fast and determinedly, but failing to become drunk. The wine brought no warmth, no release from the black bitterness that seized his mind. He cursed, hurling his glass at the smoking fire and unswept hearth. No servant would come near when his lordship was in this mood.

Those pathetic idiots at Branxholm Tower. Huddled about the remains of their feast, staring frog-eyed like so many terrified children. Even the king, that rotting flower of chivalry had been afraid.

Only in three faces there had been no fear. Only in three faces.

The Seannachie by the fire had sat studying him closely, his pale blue eyes vacant, almost as if blind, or an idiot. Soulis shrugged and pushed a twinge of unease to the back of his mind. The man was obviously a simpleton, a mind steeped in fancy, fine words, and little else.

But Marion Elliot, scarcely older than Gibbie, had stood firmly against him. Where armed and hardened soldiers had recoiled, there had flowed from her a strength almost to match his own, and Wat Scott by her side had caught it − and conquered his own fear.

What strength had these two to stand against his hate? Disbelieving, defying it, he knew already within his heart the answer.

It was love.

It was the love which all his life he had refused to admit. The love denied him by his father, and lost to him when his mother died at his birth. In that room at Branxholm he had seen love stand firm against him.

Wat and Marion between them had an awesome strength.

Soulis roamed back and forth like a caged tiger, one thought only in his mind. He must make that strength his own. He must destroy Wat and make Marion Elliot love him. With the power of love and hate combined he would have the strength of a god.

The compulsion grew. Marion must be his. Forsaking Scott, she must share with him that strength she held. But Soulis, who could create fear and hate so easily, knew no way to create love. He had returned to Hermitage and called forth the ultimate source of his power to help him, and the Dark Lord had vowed that Marion Elliot should fall within his grasp.

And so she had, that very day, so easily in the enchanted summer wood.

But hold her as he might, it was against her will and he could in no way change her mind. For hours he had first pleaded, then raged and threatened. Marion had fought him like a wild cat, her will pitted against his, defying him at every turn.

Gibbie had watched with growing and secret delight. He had stood by as she spat in the face of the man who held her prisoner, scorning his offers of wealth and position. Gibbie had seen too that all the while she clung tightly to the little wooden cross that hung about her neck, as though there lay the source of her strength.

Soulis had seen it too, and longed to tear that cross from her throat. He had tried, but each time found the hand that reached towards her fighting against some force stronger than evil. His feelings raged, confused. His longing to hurt her was pushed aside by an even stronger need to have her love, freely given.

For the first time, Gibbie and the men around Soulis saw his strength defied, his confidence shaken, and in Marion's defiance they lost a little of their own fear. They withdrew before her uneasily, superstition and awe clouding even their terror of Soulis.

At last, in desperation, Soulis had dragged her kicking and struggling to the dungeon stair. None of the men dared try to stop him, but none would have helped, except Gibbie. For once, without a word of protest, without even a kick or curse from Soulis, he stepped forward, raising a torch to light their path.

Unable to touch, or speak with Marion, he had willed his strength to join with hers. He looked her full in the face at last as Soulis unlocked the door of the secret chamber and, with a sudden shock of hope, Marion saw in the boy's expression the only promise of friendship in that place.

Her last sight of Gibbie as Soulis dragged her into the cellar, was the boy's hand, pointing and forming the sign of the cross. She stumbled to her knees, reaching blindly for the wooden crucifix, gasping in the stifling air.

Soulis stepped forward, arms outstretched, toward the chest.

'Spirit, I come.'

At last, Marion's fingers caught in the line of cord and found the cross. She pressed it tightly in her two hands, fingers locked around it.

'Come, Marion, you must help me!' She knelt at his feet, shaking her head in defiance. In frustration Soulis turned again to the chest.

'Spirit, . . .'

'Mortal!' The booming voice vibrated through them. 'Mortal, why have you summoned me before the time commanded?'

'Spirit, I beg you, one last favour.'

'No more, Soulis. No more. Thou hast had thy last. A warning only I would give to thee . . . beware the coming wood . . . the coming wood . . .'

'Spirit! Hear me! You must hear me.' He dragged Marion forward. 'This woman, Marion Elliot. You promised me, and she is here, but I would have her love . . .'

At that last word, never before uttered in that evil place, the walls and floor trembled. A screaming, as if loosed from the throats of all the devils in hell filled the vault. Soulis howled in torment. Marion, clutching the cross, lifted it to her lips.

'*In nomine Patris, et Filii, et Spiritus Sancti . . .*' she prayed, as the screaming rose to fill her whole being. She fell to the floor and remembered no more until she awoke again to find herself lying on the bed in the locked tower room, her hands still firmly clasped around the cross.

Since that time nobody had come near in answer to her shouts. She had knelt by the bed praying frantically. She had watched, helpless, as Soulis and his men prepared for the attack that

71

Wat must surely lead. She had covered her eyes in horror to see those men storm out like hornets from the rotting hive of Hermitage, knowing that it must lead to death or capture for Wat, for who could stand against a power drawn from the lord of hell himself. She huddled on the bed watching the tiny square of the window darken into night.

'Wat, Wat,' she whispered, willing her thoughts to fly to him. 'Turn back. Turn back and forget me for ever.' She would sooner have faced a life imprisoned forever in Hermitage than put his at risk.

'Pray God, Marion,' he had said, leaving her to join the king. 'Pray God.' And she did, over and over, saying to herself the words she had always known, learned in warmth of childhood and days filled with love and happiness.

**Seven**

*Hopes and fears*

Marion had no idea how long she slept, it might have been minutes, or hours. Broken by nightmare and wakefulness, time seemed endless.

In the darkest hours before the dawn a sudden tiny sound, close at hand, brought her out of a half-sleep.

Rats?

There had been rats in the dungeon, scrabbling on the edge of the blackness around them. She shivered, remembering that awful place.

The sound came again, regular and constant, tap-tap, tap-tap, tap-tap, from the direction of the bolted door. On the other side something, or someone, waited, Marion crept forward, the stool in one hand, the cross in the other, her only protection against the real or supernatural threat. Who knew what horrors Soulis bred in this ghastly den. Holding the cross firm she placed it against the rough timbers of the door.

'Stay your hand, evil spirit,' she whispered

hoarsely. 'For the Holy Cross comes between us.'

Gibbie's voice from the other side of the door brought her to her knees, her heart thumping with relief.

'Have no fear, Mistress Elliot. I would help you.'

Friendship out of the darkness, the hand in the cellar forming the sign of the cross.

'Why? Why? Are you not one of his people?'

'I . . . I no longer know, Mistress Elliot. I thought I was – my mother told me so, but . . .'

'Who are you boy?'

'Gilbert de Soulis, my lady. Half-brother to the Lord of Liddesdale. Kin to this house.'

'But no kin surely to its evil ways.'

Confusion raged in Gibbie's mind. In Marion's presence an instinct for humanity had battled with the long years of pride and arrogance in his Soulis blood, fostered by his mother's teaching.

'You are no kin, Gibbie! Your soul would stand against his. I saw that in your eyes, and so must Soulis. Gibbie! Are you still there?'

'Yes . . . yes . . .'

'Then tell me now, for you must know, he has admitted you to his secrets. Tell me, Gibbie. Is it possible to break his power? In God's name, Gibbie, I beg you! I have little strength left to fight.'

She placed the flat of her hand against the door, as if reaching out to touch him.

'Gibbie. Before it is too late, the choice is yours to make. Turn from this evil. Help me – please!'

And in that instant Gibbie chose. It was as if an iron band, placed there at birth, had been taken from around his head. He laughed, strangely, shaking with the sense of freedom.

'I am here, Mistress Elliot, and with you. Guard your strength, for I have seen that he may be fought. With help we may bring him down.'

'With whose help Gibbie? The king fears him. What mortal man may stand against him? Wat – Wat will try . . .'

'But cannot stop him,' hissed Gibbie. 'He can never win. Soulis fights with the Old Evil from the Darkness of the Six Nights of Creation. It would take a man versed in the Old Knowledge to match his power.'

'And is there one such to be found?'

'There is one man, perhaps.' Gibbie's voice was urgent now and low. Servants were beginning to wake in the castle. 'I have seen him stand before Soulis as you did. And I have seen signs . . .'

'Who, Gibbie, *who*?'

'The Seannachie, Mistress Elliot. Thomas the Storyteller, the rhymer. He has a casket.'

'The Seannachie?' she breathed, incredulous. The slow, gentle man with the soft honeyed voice. That tall, quiet man who wore the faded blue robe of the ballad-maker. The soft summer-blue eyes that seemed always fixed on some

75

distant world, but which missed nothing.

'Thomas the Storyteller?'

'The Storyteller. I believe he has the secret of the Old Knowledge that may bring down Soulis.'

'Then you must find him. Go to him, Gibbie! Go now before the men return. Seek him, seek him and bring him to Hermitage!'

'I would, my lady, I would. But it means that I must leave you here with him – alone.'

'It matters little what happens to me, Gibbie, but Soulis must be destroyed. Go, Gibbie, go now!'

She could feel the boy's reluctance. Turning to go, he hesitated. Fear rose, choking in Marion's throat at the thought that she must send away this one lifeline, her only friend within the castle. But love for Wat rose even stronger, containing and imprisoning that fear. It might be that she could still save him somehow.

'Go quickly, Gibbie, leave now while it is still dark and none are watching. Ride to the king, the Seannachie is with him. Go with my love and blessing – and with God's.'

She pressed her palm flat against the door, and Gibbie placing his own on the other side, took his leave.

'Fare you well, Mistress Elliot. Have courage, and hold fast until I return.'

He tapped once more  softly on the door and

vanished silently, leaving the silence to settle around Marion like a pall.

Within the hour it was shattered by shouts from the courtyard. She leapt to the window. Surely they had not caught the boy already. He must have escaped. He must win through to freedom and find the Seannachie. She clawed frantically at the shutter, no longer caring whether or not they saw her.

The returning men formed a ring in the courtyard, laughing and shouting. Their voices echoed wildly from the walls. From the flashing, unsheathed swords and their breathless excitement, Marion knew that they had drawn blood, and had won.

Into the centre of the ring stepped Soulis. She knew him instantly by the streak of white against the jet black hair. He turned, staring up at the tower window where he knew she must be watching and the light fell full on his triumphant hate-filled face.

Still watching her window, he waved his arm. Two men stepped forward, dragging between them a heavy bundle wrapped in a blood-stained cloak. Soulis snatched at the cloak, hauling it aside.

The limp body of Wat Scott sprawled like an old rag doll on the cobbles, dried blood congealing on his forehead.

Drowning in a wave of despair, Marion fell to her knees weeping bitterly.

# Eight

## The devil's bonfire

Allan Elliot wandered blindly down the wind-swept beach to the sea.

The water, whipped to a restless mood by the rising wind, swept in grey curling waves on to the wet sand of the tide line. Out across the bay, rain clouds had been gathering all morning, gradually blotting out the distant blue peaks of the island of Arran. The soft green hills of the headland dissolved in a sudden squall of rain. Allan turned away from the stinging needles of the dry blown sand of the high dunes, his cheeks glistening.

The cry of a lonely storm-tossed gull echoed back his grief. The world wept with him.

He hunched his shoulders against the west wind from the sea and watched the squall sweep across the town of Ayr, the cluster of houses around the high stone tower of the old church. Like a mother hen with chicks. Up on the south headland, alone above the harbour, stood the castle where, since the news of Marion's capture and Wat's ambush, argument had swept endlessly and aimlessly back and forward.

'Hermitage must be taken and Soulis destroyed now!' the duke raged, his face purple with fury and emotion. 'We maun waste no more time.'

The others round the table, strong powerful men, nodded in agreement. The king, having fought so hard to unite this group about him, sensed already that he was losing their support. Whatever differences and jealousies they might have had in the past, they were united in their loathing of Soulis, and would follow the old duke to the death.

But still Robert hesitated.

'I will summon him – summon him to come before me and account for his actions. There will be a trial, I promise you, but he must be judged before his equals.'

The duke stormed to his feet, a huge fist crashing down on the table rattling plates and goblets.

'Equals! he has no equals! Unless ye have it in mind to invite all the de'ils of hell about ye. Summon him would you? You would have us kindly invite this . . . this scum . . . this blot on the face of God's good earth, to join us! And all the while my son and his lass . . .'

Choking for words he collapsed into his chair, suddenly old beyond his years and sick to the heart. At his side Richard Elliot, Marion's father, nodded in silent agreement, grey-faced and paralysed in hopeless inaction. The murmur of dissent around the table grew to a louder wave of protest.

The king rose to his feet and faced them stubbornly, with the argument he had used over and over.

'He is *my* kin. As such he is of royal blood. You have no right to demand the life of one who stands close in line to the throne. Think, my lords, if anything should happen to my son . . .'

'It will be of his doing,' snapped the duke. 'My lord you *must* destroy this fiend, before he destroys you too. For *all* our sakes.'

But still Robert hesitated to give his agreement.

Unable any longer to bear the rage and torment, Allan had stormed out of the hall and had come at last to the edge of the sea.

He wept for Marion. He wept for Wat, big gentle Wat, close as a brother. Wat with his rare flashes of wild temper, and even wilder flashes of fun when the mood took him.

He wept for his father, no man of war, whose days were spent in constant work among his crops and beasts. Strong, dependable, coping in all weathers through good times and bad, he sat now sunk helpless in grief. He wept too for his mother at home with friends and family to build a wall of comfort and support about her. And yet he knew, because he felt it too, that within that wall she stood alone, imprisoned in the agony no others could share.

And the fault was his!

He lifted his head and cried a great howl of anger and frustration into the wind. Soulis must be stopped! Of that there could be no doubt, but the king, who must stop him, swithered aimlessly and the others argued like spiteful children.

Allan lifted a stick from the sand and flung it furiously as far out into the grey water as he could, then turning on his heel he strode back up into the town, raging inwardly.

It was as if all the evil and hate of the world, spreading like cancer from Hermitage, infected each one it touched, leaving them weak and unable to fight the killing disease. There must be a way, and it must be found soon.

He wandered past the scattered fishermen's cottages along the sandy shore, heading towards the great square tower of the church, and the cosy, dirty huddle of houses around the Mercat Cross and the old toll bridge.

Here and there a head turned to watch him as he passed. One of the gentry they noted, mentally pricing the fine woollen cloak and the sword. Their sharp eyes missed nothing. They brought with them only fighting and trouble, or demands for more taxes. Best to leave them alone.

They turned back to their work, or called to enquire of a neighbour the reason for the stir about the Mercat Cross. The shouting had drifted across on the wind, the words difficult to catch.

'Is it the mummers come to town?' they asked. But the mummers – acrobats, actors and clowns – came with the Lammas Fair and there were weeks of harvest still before that.

'It'll be a fight, no doubt.'

The shouts rose in volume, jeers and catcalls echoing among them. It was no ordinary fight.

'It's a witch!' The words went round like a heath fire. Fascinated horror fanned the flames of gossip. There had been a deal of talk of witchcraft in the town. Only the week before they had burned two old women at Irvine up the coast where there had been an outbreak of fever and men, women and children had fallen dying in the streets.

Ayr, so far, was safe, and the citizens intended to keep it that way. No man would lift a hand to defend a suspected witch against the fury of this mob.

'They say the soldiers have caught themselves a warlock! They mean to burn him at the Cross.'

A burning. It had been a long time since the last one in Ayr. Nets dropped unmended, looms fell silent, bannocks scorched on baking stones as the word spread and they flocked to the market square by the old toll bridge.

'Fetch a priest!' the cry went up. 'We maun do this right and proper.'

'My, but he's an evil sight, right enough, and him just a wee bit laddie. Would you believe it?' screeched an old woman, straining for a better view.

'You had best believe it, old wife,' shouted one of the soldiers. 'This fiend of hell learned his trade at the hands of the master, Soulis himself.'

The woman crossed herself. The crowd fell back awe-struck at the name.

Soulis!

Pushed and jostled on all sides by people struggling to reach the cross, Allan caught the name and stopped in his tracks. He grabbed wildly at the nearest passer-by, a stout man in the greasy leather apron of a blacksmith.

'What's that they're saying? Is it Soulis they hold?'

The big man pulled back, wary of the red-rimmed, staring eyes.

'No sir, no.' He barged off into the crowd. 'It's just one of his men.' Allan struggled after him, elbowing heedlessly through the seething mass.

A skirl of hatred rose from the crowd as the soldiers forced a way through to the stone platform by the cross, dragging with them a shouting, struggling boy. Already, willing hands were gathering together brushwood and sticks to build the witch-fire. Bundles of kindling were passed from hand to hand over the heads of the people and a howl went up each time the pile grew.

'Higher! Higher! Higher!'

Allan fought and kicked his way through them. He must get to the boy before they killed him. If he had really come from Soulis he might have word of Marion and Wat.

Gasping, he struggled to the front of the crowd in time to see the soldiers haul their warlock up on to the heap of wood and bind his arms firmly behind his back.

'Now, my fine laddie, face your accusers!' snarled one of the soldiers. He grabbed the long dark hair and pulled the boy's head up. The face was white and drawn, the wild dark eyes hunting the crowd for some hope of rescue or escape.

It was the boy – the boy, Gibbie, who rode with Soulis, who was said to be with him day and night, privy to his evil practices.

'Stop!' Allan's voice was lost in the screaming frenzy. 'Stop! We must take him to the king!'

Gibbie, tied hand and foot, struggled to plead with the howling crowd.

'Listen to me. You must listen to me . . .' They jeered and spat at him, seeing only a hated enemy begging cravenly for his life. He turned wildly to the soldier nearest him.

'I *beg* you, take me to the king.' The big man roared with laughter.

'Did you hear that?' he bellowed to the raging crowd. 'He wants to see the king. He says I must take him.' The bellow of rage rose to a crescendo.

'He would practise his evil arts on the King – and I'M TO TAKE HIM THERE!' He struck out, knocking the boy to his knees. The crowd bayed for more. This was turning out to be an even more memorable burning than the last, when the witch had been a daft, insensible old woman with no fight left in her.

'A torch, a torch!' screamed a voice. 'Burn him now!'

'Burn him now! Burn him now!' The chorus was taken up by the others.

'Burn him! Let's see the bonny fire he'll make.'

'A torch! A torch!'

'In God's name STOP!' screamed Allan. 'Hold back your fire. The king must see him.'

'Master Elliot,' Gibbie's voice was hoarse now with shouting. 'Help me . . . master . . .help me . . . I have seen your sister . . .'

'Where is she? What has he done with her?'

'Here's another one,' howled the big soldier, mad with power and hardly believing his luck. He seized Allan by the shoulder hauling him up to face the crowd. 'These two are acquaint it would seem. It may be they're both in league with the devil!'

A yell went up from the crowd, whipped to a frenzy by the soldiers. Two burnings at the one

85

time! Such a thing had never been known that any of them could remember.

'Burn them both! Light the Devil's Bonfire!'

'It's not true . . . NO!' Allan fought and kicked against the men who pinned him down, tying his hands. 'It's not true. I swear it. Gibbie, tell them . . .'

'Listen to him,' screamed a woman. 'He's no' one of us. He talks with the same ill-tongue as yon evil creature there. Burn the both of them.'

'Burn them, burn them, burn them . . .' chanted the crowd.

They dragged Allan to his feet, and bound him back to back with Gibbie. He fought helplessly, craning for a sight of a face from the castle in that seething crowd. But there was none. Instead he saw only the townspeople, surging ever closer, piling around his feet the bundles of dried brushwood and kindling, higher and higher. He caught in his throat the acrid smoke of the torches held high, passed from the ring of houses around the square. Terrified, he opened his mouth to shout and found his voice suffocating in a dry throat. From behind him came Gibbie's voice.

'Master Elliot – your sister – she was safe when I left her.'

'Where?'

'Hermitage. In the tower room above the gateway.'

'And Wat . . . what has he done with Wat?'

The answer was lost in the howl of the mob as the first torch was thrust into the damp brushwood. Gibbie's voice came through the screaming, chanting softly, steadily – unknown words of prayer, witchcraft – or both.

The tiny flames caught hold, and licking from twig to twig swept round them. Already Allan could feel the heat of their burning, the thick smoke choking his lungs and blinding his eyes.

'NO MORE! NO MORE!'

The powerful voice, carrying above all others, roared out over the crowd. Blinking back tears and gasping for breath, Allan squinted through the smoke. Behind him Gibbie slowly raised his lowered head, eyes closed, smiling. His prayer or incantation had been answered.

An eerie silence crept over the crowd. Slowly they parted and through the gap, walking tall and majestic as any king, came Thomas the Seannachie. Looking neither to right of left he climbed the stone platform on which the fire was set. Neither heat nor smoke seemed to trouble him. In his hands he held the strangely patterned little chest.

The rabble fell silent. The soldiers, recognising a man who had the ear of the king, stepped down from the fire. Ignoring them, Thomas faced the crowd and raising the casket above his head chanted in a voice that carried over the rooftops to the very storm clouds gathering above them.

'No more I say. The wrath of Heaven descends on those who would destroy an innocent life!'

Three times he flourished the chest above his head and repeated the words, turning each time to a different section of the crowd. As he raised the chest for the third time a blinding flash of lightning split the heavy clouds. Thunder crashed about them and rumbled deafeningly out to sea. The crowd fled as the heavens opened and rain lashed down in torrents, and still the Seannachie stood defying the elements.

'I knew he would help, Master Elliot. I knew he would hear me and help . . .' Gibbie laughed wildly as the rain plastered the fine dark hair about his face. Around their feet the hissing fire died in the battering rainstorm.

Allan Elliot stood silent as Thomas cut the ropes that bound him to Gibbie. He watched awestruck as Gibbie and the Seannachie, coming face to face, raised each his left hand and brought them together finger-tip to finger-tip. Gibbie's long thin transparent fingers against the strong brown ones.

'What seek you, boy?'

'Aid, from one who has the power.'

'How know you of this?'

'I too have felt it, master.'

'Soulis has the power . . .'

'But yours is stronger.'

Allan stared from one to the other as, unaware of his presence they spoke the strange catechism.

'His power is potent, boy, it is the power of the Six Nights of Creation and the deeds that dare not be seen by God's Light.'

'But yours is stronger still master. Yours is the power born of the Six Days of Creation and Soulis fears it.'

'Strong enough for that which has been foretold, but we shall see, we shall see.' He stared at Gibbie, long and hard, then shaking his head seemed suddenly to make a decision.

'I shall need help. With love and faith my power will be the more potent. But I need also one I may trust. These three shall stand against Soulis.'

'Love there is already in plenty, and faith. And I swear, master, on the life of my everlasting soul, you may trust me.'

The Seannachie nodded, seeing in the boy who stood before him the fulfilling of the old prophecy.

*'There will come to you a boy capable of great good or evil . . .'*

'Come then,' he said, reaching out a hand, 'for the day is already wasting,' Laying an arm round Gibbie's shoulder he led the boy down from the awful place of death towards a new life.

Allan stumbled after them, confused, only half-understanding the words he had heard.

In the castle the argument came to a conclusion. Robert paced the hall like a wild beast, facing his hunters. He paused by the window, his back to them, gazing out across the sea at his beloved island of Arran, half-hidden through the clearing mists. There had been a time when the island had saved him. He had lived then a hunted man, hiding from the enemy as they swept through his land seeking to find and destroy the growing fires of resistance and independence. He had lived rough in caves and on hillsides. They had been dangerous times, and yet easier in some ways than these. Knowing himself beaten he turned with a sigh to face the group, led by the duke, who sat stone-faced around the table.

The walls shook around them. Lightning flashed, sudden and vivid across each frozen face, thunder crashing in their ears. A shutter smashed back on its hinges as the summer storm, sweeping in from the sea, broke over the castle.

Robert's fraying temper shattered suddenly with the release of tension in the room. He snatched up the pen and, scrawling his name on the document his Council had drawn up, finally pronounced the Doom of Soulis.

He hurled the pen into the heart of the fire and stormed out of the room, his voice roaring through the castle.

'You can boil him if you will, my lords, but trouble me no more!'

# Nine

## The coming wood

Marion sat wrapped in one coarse blanket, feeling neither the cold, nor damp nor the hardness of the stone floor. Huddled in the corner, unaware of hunger or pain, her whole being was concentrated into one image in her mind. Closed or open her eyes saw only Wat, lying sprawled on the cobbles of the courtyard and the gloating face of Soulis. His eyes had seemed to bore into her very soul.

Was he dead? Was he alive? Marion willed herself to believe in Wat warm and living. She willed herself to remember his voice, and the grip of his strong brown hands. The feel and smell of his hair against her cheek. She could see him laughing with Allan. Her mother used to say that laugh of Wat's would scare the hens off laying, such a wild joyful shout. How often she had teased him about it.

Tears stung her eyes, choking in her throat.

'Gibbie!' The shout shattered the images in her mind. 'Gibbie! Where are you, you worthless

92

snivelling runt! Find him!'

So Soulis knew his half-brother was missing. She crawled to the door and knelt, hardly breathing, pressing her ear against the crack. Running footsteps pounded on the stairs, followed by others. In the depths of the castle, doors slammed, bolts creaked and clanged open.

'Not here, my lord.'

'Nor here.'

'Find him! Hunt the brat down and bring him here. NOW!'

Shouted questions rang back and forth. Rooms were ransacked, the castle searched from kitchens to battlements. The hunt was up, but of Gibbie there seemed to be no sign. Marion could feel the mood of anger spreading from Soulis to the shouts of the men. But they hunted in vain.

He must have escaped before their return.

Oh please God, she prayed, he had gone far enough and fast enough to lose them.

He must win through to the king and find the Seannachie. He must.

She leapt to her feet with a start as the heavy wooden bolt fell back with a clatter. The door crashed open and she stood face to face with the Lord of Liddesdale.

The elegant expensive clothes hung dirty and disordered, the exquisite hands were filthy, nails broken as if he had himself torn the castle apart in his search for Gibbie. His face seemed slacker, the black eyes were sunken and dull. He had the look about him of sleepless days and nights, a man tormented by waking dreams, haunted by fears.

But still Soulis was no less dangerous. He stood poised like a cornered wild cat in the doorway.

Marion's fingers closed around the cross, carefully and without seeming to move. He sensed it.

'You seek to frighten me with your infant superstitions.' His smile was chilling, but he came no closer. Marion saw, suddenly, behind the cruelty, a glimmer of doubt in his eyes. She raised the cross higher.

'You *will* not harm me, you *dare* not harm me my lord.'

'Where is Gibbie?' he snarled. 'He has gone at your bidding, I know it. Whom does he seek?'

'My lord, you hold me prisoner here. What would I know of your servants?'

'He has spoken with you. I know it. I saw in his face that he would.'

Marion said nothing. Her eyes held his boldly, fear thumping in her chest.

'He has betrayed me. You have sent him for help. *Whom does he seek?*'

She shook her head, defying him, and backed away as he approached.

'Not the king. It is not the king for he is useless. No. He seeks another power. I feel it. Who — who is it?' His voice was soft and threatening.

'You cannot harm me, my lord. I have God's blessing and protection, and the love of my kinsmen who will surely . . .'

'Kinsmen!' he snapped. His movements seemed strange, jerky and unpredictable. 'Kinsmen! Those dung-spreading peasants will come after me, do you say? I shall show you what lies in store for them.'

He turned towards the door shouting for his men.

'Cling to your cross, my holy one, while you may. A pity that your beloved does not share the same protection.'

Marion stepped back with a scream as two men entered dragging between them the limp body of Wat. They dumped him on the floor at her feet and Soulis waved them impatiently from the room.

He stood by the door watching her. Marion on her knees beside Wat, already cradling his head in her arms, saw beyond the hatred to a strange longing. For the length of a heatbeat he stood, then, seeing mirrored in her eyes the knowledge of his weakness, he slammed out, bolting the door behind him.

'Enjoy what little time you have, madam, for I have ensured that he still lives. Come sunset I will take you both out and hang you!'

Marion heard neither the bolt crash home, nor Soulis's footsteps fading down the stairwell. She knew only that Wat was alive, saw the bruised blue eyelids flicker and the cracked blood-streaked lips whisper her name.

He still lived. The word had gone out from Soulis that Wat was to be brought back to Hermitage alive at all costs. The blow on his head, though enough to knock him senseless, was superficial.

Those same words drummed through the head of Wat's father as he rode wildly at the head of a large group of armed men.

They still lived. They still lived. He refused to let himself believe otherwise. The pounding beat of the hooves hammered the words into his brain. Riding hard by day and night he had led his men by the course of the Doon, south across the high mosses of Galloway, where the smell of the sea mingled fresh and keen with the scent of the bracken. They pounded through tiny villages, and mothers, seeing the approaching cloud of dust, snatched their children from the path of the king's men and barricaded themselves in their cottages. They had seen enough killing in the bad times when men had left their wives and children never to return. Crops had lain rotting in the fields and beast were driven off by the soldiers. So they huddled behind barred doors as the duke and his men passed.

Let the fine lords fight their own wars, they

wanted none of it.

The duke galloped on, driven by revenge and pausing only to take fresh horses from the king's castle of Lochmaben. They swept north along the blue stretch of the Solway Firth and came at last through Gretna to Canonbie. There, beneath the shoulder of Bruntshiel, where the Rowan Burn met the Liddel Water, others waited for them. Armed with swords, pitchforks or staves, they came from Hawick, Teviot and Liddesdale. Men who had lived too long under the terrifying shadow of Hermitage.

Little talk passed between them, each man preparing himself to meet an enemy of fearsome strength. They were led by the best and bravest of the men who supported the king, but in each heart was real fear, and in each mind the blessing bestowed on them by the king's priests at their leaving.

Would it be strong enough to protect them? Could faith and the blessing of a distant priest help them stand against Soulis? There were those who doubted it, but doubting it still they followed the duke, strong in their loyalty to him and Wat.

As if by some alchemy, that strength carried to Wat and Marion as they waited. These hours together seemed the longest and yet the shortest they would ever spend. Wat's first thought on coming on his senses had been to find some means of escape. With only the stool as a weapon he battered at the door, but the rotten wood broke in his hands and he was left holding the stump of a leg.

Wat tried with Marion's help to use the jagged wood to prise the heavy iron bolt from the shutter, but it proved impossible. The men in the courtyard watching them laughed raucously and hurled abusive suggestions. He hurled down the piece of rotten wood and turned back to the room.

'Help me tear these wall-hangings into strips, Marion. We'll make a rope and climb out of here!' The rotten tapestries tore easily, but would never have held their weight and the drop to the heavily guarded courtyard was a long one.

In frustration Wat went back to battering the door with his bare hands.

The afternoon wore on. The patch of sunlight from the window slid inexorably across the floor, their only clock. Stop, prayed Marion silently. Oh stop! If only she could hold time in her hands and keep forever these precious hours. She wept a little then for what might have been.

Giving what comfort he could, Wat held her close in his arms, remembering the years they had known each other. He saw himself again as a small boy by his mother's bedside. She had died giving birth to a tiny sister who had lived only a few hours and then followed her. The grief had been devastating but gradually he had left it behind in sharing with Allan the baby sister born that same day to Mistress Elliot.

He held her close and gently stroked her hair.

'They will come, Marion.' He put a firmness and courage into his voice that he scarcely felt. 'They will come.'

The day wore on towards evening. The thundery summer heat was oppressive in the tiny room. A sullen quiet hung over the castle. In the courtyard footsteps were few and muffled, voices low. Men met and passed as if afraid to look in each other's eyes and see there the enormity of the crime about to be committed.

The look-out, posted to watch the road through Liddesdale and the bleak moorland passes, came and went having seen no trace of any pursuit. Soulis paced his hall, the even tread of his steps like a clock ticking away the hours.

'Nothing to report, my lord. The road lies clear still.'

'Enough!' He finally exploded in a storm of temper. 'These cowards would hunt in stealth like the rats of the cesspit. Then my hounds will seek them out.' He called together a group of his men, the most trusted and ruthless of all.

'They come seeking me – and you must stop them.'

'But my lord, the road is empty . . .' The man staggered back, felled by a savage blow.

'Fool! I tell you I *know* they come. I have seen it.'

In silence they saddled up and, heavily armed, rode out to hunt down the duke and his men. Soulis watched them go, and still he paced. Now the battlements, now the courtyard, he roamed the castle like some demented trapped beast. Watching him, it seemed to Wat and Marion almost as if he and not they were the prisoner.

He paused neither to eat nor drink. No servant offered any, they skulked in kitchen and cellar fearing to face his rage.

In the cool of the long afternoon, as the sun was sinking, the hoofbeats of a single horse came to them faintly, thudding wildly on the dusty road. A man riding for his life. Wat and Marion watched by the window as the horse clattered madly through the low gateway into the courtyard, hooves sparking on the cobbles, and the man fell gasping at his master's feet. His helmet sword and shield had gone. Across the breast of his leather tunic a dark spreading stain soaked out his life. The left arm hung useless, blood dripping from the fingers. He struggled to haul himself to his knees.

'My lord . . . my lord . . .'

'The others? Where are the others?' Soulis stood before him, taut as a bowstring.

'Dead, my lord, all dead . . .' The man reached out a hand, reeling from lack of blood. Soulis made no move to help him.

'What happened, imbecile? Tell me!' The man

swallowed and tried to speak, blood trickling from his lips.

'In the gully along the river bank, where the trees grow thick . . . they came upon us . . . beware . . .' Soulis seized the man's hair, and kneeling by his side, turned the tortured face up to the light.

'Again . . . again . . . louder, fool!'

'Beware . . . beware the coming . . . the coming wood!' The man's voice faded tonelessly as he slumped dead on the cobbles.

The coming wood. The coming wood . . . Those words that only he and Gibbie and the girl had heard in the dungeon. And yet this fool repeated them in his dying breath.

Beware the coming wood.

High in the tower room neither Wat nor Marion heard the man's words. They saw only that Soulis threw him to the ground, starting back as if driven by some powerful blow, his whole body recoiling against it. They heard him howl in a voice scarcely recognisable to those of his men who remained.

'Bring them to me!' He faced their window, his power so strong they stepped back almost as if hit by a wave. 'Bring them to me! Since they are so consumed with the desire to be everlastingly united I will help them to that end – in DEATH!'

# Ten

## The casket

In the hour of gloaming, the northern summer dim that is neither night nor day, the woods around Hermitage lay still and breathless.

No bird sang in the leafy branches, no mouse rustled, hunting in the undergrowth for food. It was as if the creatures of the earth retreated before the presence of Soulis.

Up the Liddel Water, to the east of the castle by the edge of the wood stood a huge oak tree. Older than any in the forest it had been full grown in the time of that first Lord Soulis who had come to Hermitage from France bringing with him unknown words and dragging on a ramshackle cart the chest that lay in the dungeon.

The oak now stood, leafless and barren. The rotting branches, outwardly strong, a warren of worm and maggot, eating out the heart of the once great tree. From the dead twigless branches the fungus grew, rich and gorgeous, but crumbling at the touch of a finger.

A magpie perched expectantly on the topmost branch.

Soulis stood on the hummock of rank grass beneath the tree to face his prisoners. No trace now of weakness, he seemed his old self again, hard and determined. His men had hauled Wat and Marion before him, hands tied behind their backs. They stood now side by side, as if bride and groom before some perverted priest. And there was in the face of Soulis something of the look of a man of religion, intense and burning.

'I ask you now, one last time, Marion Elliot. Agree to be my wife and I will spare the life of this peasant and send him packing to his pig-sty.'

'No, Marion, in God's name, no!' Wat struggled against the ropes.

'Refuse to dance at my wedding and you will dance at your own − at the end of a rope.'

Marion spat at the feet of Soulis.

'That for your offer of marriage Soulis. Take Wat's life, take mine, for it is worthless to me without him.'

'You will not have me for a husband? Think then what you have lost. You might have been mistress of Hermitage − and of the kingdom, by my side, for the crown is mine and none shall stop me.'

'I would as soon reign in hell.'

'Then have me for a priest! For I will celebrate your marriage. I will bind you together with this ass and you may hang side by side on the same branch.' Madness sparked in his eyes and on his flushed cheeks. Even his men recoiled in horror at the thought of hanging a woman.

'Animal! Even your evil cannot possibly . . .' Wat burst out in fury, but Marion, tied though she was, turned to his side.

'If we cannot live together, at least we may die together,' she said calmly. 'For that at least I thank you.'

Soulis seethed in cold rage, his eyes burning.

'The ropes! Bring me the ropes! I shall hang them here before my own battlements that I may have the pleasure of seeing them rot day by day.'

In the creeping darkness of the coming night ropes were fetched and tossed over a high branch. Above their heads clouds gathered across the face of the rising moon, and deep in the trees a distant owl hooted, low and eerie. Wat and Marion were dragged beneath the tree.

'My love . . .' whispered Marion as a noose was placed about each neck. The owl's call echoed her whisper, closer at hand now. Beside her she felt Wat stiffen. The man holding him turned at a half-heard rustle in the bushes. Around them the wood seemed thicker and closer. Their eyes played tricks in the fading light. The bushes rustled again.

Soulis froze, watching. Against the black tunic his face and hands glowed luminous in the eerie light. It was only a wind, a light evening wind, stirring the undergrowth.

'Hang them,' he snarled, snapping his fingers. 'I would see them dance before me!'

But there was no wind.

Too late the man holding Wat realised and heard the bushes rustle again. Too late, he saw, but failed to understand, what was happening.

'My lord?' The rising panic was clear in his voice. 'My lord? The wood . . . the wood comes towards us!' He turned from Wat, drawing his sword as the bushes did indeed seem to come closer.

The words rang a death knell in the heart of Soulis, an echo from the dungeon.

'Beware the coming wood – beware the coming wood . . .'

He had scarcely time to shout a warning and draw his own sword when they fell upon him. The duke and his men, creeping up under cover of broken branches, had completely surrounded them. The clearing rang to the screams of dying and wounded men, the clash of swords and spears.

The fight, like a fire raging out of control, was too violent to last long. At the end, surrounded by the fallen bodies of the men who had stood by him, cursing those who had fled into the forest, Soulis stood, disarmed, with his back to the tree from whose branches he would have hung Wat and Marion.

Disarmed, but unharmed, for each man's sword had fallen useless against him. Wat, untied, seized Allan's sword. He stepped forward, and lunging with all the strength left in him, aimed straight at the heart of Soulis. The blade shattered and fell broken between. As before at Branxholm the power of Soulis defied revenge.

'Try what you will, my pretty lad,' he sneered laughing. 'You cannot destroy me. Sword cannot harm, rope hang, nor fire burn.'

The duke stepped forward, lashing out in a rage, but his sword too, splintering like glass, fell useless. They stood, father, brother and friends, merciless in their hate, yet powerless, and he knew it.

Slowly he bent to pick up his own sword.

'I fear I am beyond your petty power, my lords.'

'But not mine – Soulis – not mine!'

The smile froze on the lips of Soulis. His words hung dying in the air.

From the darkness of the forest, his eyes shining in the half-light, stepped Thomas the Seannachie, and at his side, bearing in his arms the curiously-patterned chest, stood Gibbie.

'You did not ride with us!' The duke's voice was a strangled whisper, his men stood amazed.

Neither Soulis nor the Seannachie were aware

106

of their consternation. They faced each other across the clearing. Gibbie stood between them, tense, as if waiting for what must happen. Soulis, his eyes fixed on the Seannachie, his face a deathly white mask of loathing, snarled viciously.

'Traitor, Gilbert de Soulis, traitor . . .'

'De Soulis!' blurted the duke. 'That lad's another cub of the devil?' But the Seannachie raised his hand for silence. The boy stepped forward. Like Thomas he, too, seemed to have taken on an air of authority, and to be not quite of this world.

The Seannachie crossed the clearing, the faded blue robe floating like the mist through the trees. Men parted to let him pass, awestruck. Questions half-formed died on their lips.

'How did he come here?'

'In what way? There is no horse . . .'

Soulis backed against the broad trunk of the oak tree, but still the Seannachie came on, until standing an arm's length from him he stopped. His eyes, that curious piercing faded blue of his robe, bored into the black eyes of Soulis, seeing there the evil that had to be defeated.

'Your time has come, my lord.' The voice of the storyteller was deep and resonant.

'You cannot stop me, my power is strong.'

'It may be broken by one stronger.'

'I call to my bidding the power of eternal hate. The power of the Darkness of the Six Nights of

Creation.'

'Still I say it may be broken by one stronger.' The Seannachie's voice was calm as if reasoning with a child.

'There is none stronger!'

The Seannachie swept round slowly, an arm outstretched to Wat and Marion.

'These two faced and fought your evil, with love and faith.'

'And failed! Their great love and faith had not the strength to save them in the end. I would have hung them both. No faith can stand against the power of the Darkness of the Nights of God's Sleep.'

Thomas stood silent, watching him. Then with a slow, sad smile he shook his head. In those seconds Soulis knew, beyond all certainty, that the time of his destruction had come, and felt real soul-raking fear.

Silent still, Thomas signed for Gibbie to come forward. The boy came to his side, holding out the chest.

'Scum!' snarled Soulis. 'Traitor to our name. On you might have fallen the mantle of my greatness.'

'No, brother,' said Gibbie firmly. 'I shall be the last of the House of Soulis. On my shoulders shall hang no mantle of greatness, only a yoke of guilt for the evil of past generations. It is fitting therefore that it should fall to me to make amends. And to pronounce the Doom of Soulis.'

He stood, slight beside the heavily armed men, and yet with the strength of a sapling that bends before the gale that breaks the greater trees. He held high the chest and knelt before Thomas. The storyteller's voice rose suddenly, thundering through the woods, sending birds fluttering in fear from their nests.

'Prepare, Soulis, to meet those whom you have worshipped. Come Wat, come Marion.' As they moved to his side, his fingers, like long white twigs in the gloom, slid across the curiously patterned surface of the chest, touching here and stroking there.

Slowly, slowly he lifted the lid.

Every eye in the clearing was upon him. Every heart beat faster. Gently – so gently that they were scarcely aware of it, their minds were filled with a music heard from without or within, of unbearably sad sweetness.

One by one they felt the strength and peace of the Seannachie's power flow through them, and sank to their knees.

The Seannachie and Soulis faced each other. Thomas reached into the casket and with the tips of his fingers lifted out a slab of stone, holding it before him. On it were cut symbols which burned as if drawn from the crust beneath the seething earth. Only Gibbie and the Seannachie dared face that light, heads unbowed.

109

'Come, Lord, come,' intoned the Seannachie. 'I beg in the name of all that is holy and the power born of the earth. I beg in the name of the power born of the Six Days of Creation and nurtured in God's good light. I beg in the name of the power born of love, faith and trust, these three . . .'

As he spoke the last words Gibbie, Wat and Marion each stretching out towards him, laid a hand on the stone tablet.

Around them a roaring as of a thousand volcanoes filled the shuddering bodies of the duke and his men. Birds and beasts fled screaming as the forest shook. The trees trembled as if some great wave had passed through the mossy earth beneath their feet.

'No!' screamed Soulis, his voice in the deafening hurricane unleashed by the Seannachie. 'No . . . I defy you . . . defy . . .'

Slowly the roaring died away. The pain in splitting heads faded and they breathed again.

Soulis backed transfixed against the tree, his eyes glazed in horror, facing his castle of Hermitage. From the topmost roofs of the tower, to the door which led to the dungeon of that dreadful place the stone had split open as if cracked like a nutshell.

'No . . .' he breathed, his voice rasping in his throat. 'No . . .'

Slowly the top of the tower tilted crazily. Slowly, it slipped. It seemed to those watching to hang in the air for an eternity. From deep inside the castle came a rumbling, felt in the earth, rather than heard. The huge blocks of stone crumbled, crashing downward through hall and kitchen, blocking courtyard and dungeon. Fire leapt from the ruin casting an unearthly blue glow against the darkening sky. A scream filled the air. No human voice, but so horrible and so lasting it was for ever to ring in the minds and nightmares of all those who heard it.

Soulis staggered forward, oblivious of those around him, reaching out towards the shattered castle.

'Spirit, I come!' His voice was lost in the crashing of falling masonry.

'Spirit, I come . . .' He screamed again, stretching desperate hands, as if to arms awaiting him. Tears streamed down his face.

'Spirit . . . wait . . .'

His voice choked in his throat. His face contorted in terrifying pain and horror as if he had come, finally, face to face with the ultimate unimaginable evil.

Gasping, he crumpled on the grass at the foot of the ancient rotting oak tree, his sightless eyes reflecting the flames that destroyed Hermitage. From the branches above his head a magpie flew screaming and vanished into the smoke.

Ranulf de Soulis, Lord of Liddesdale, Guardian of the King's Peace, and one time cousin of His Royal Grace, lay dead, the soul torn from his racked and tortured body.

## Eleven

## The
## Doom of
## Soulis

They stood dumbstruck as the black silence settled around them and the howling echoes died away across the wilds of Liddesdale.

Gilbert de Soulis, Lord of Liddesdale, knelt before them at the side of the half-brother whose title he must now inherit, however unwillingly.

The Seannachie looked from one to the other, his blue eyes blazing with strength and authority. Slowly he laid the stone back in the casket and gently closed the lid.

The spell that had held them faded like the morning mist.

The duke shook his head, as if emerging from a dream then, seeing Wat, stepped forward and threw his arms around him in a great crushing bear hug.

He took Marion carefully in his arms and held her as if she had been some tiny fragile bird he was afraid to hurt.

'Oh lassie . . . lassie . . .' He sniffed, his old

113

eyes glistening brightly in the dark. She hugged and kissed him.

'Wat gave me his cross. *He . . . he* seemed afraid to touch it.'

The old duke stared at the little wooden crucifix, the deathbed gift of a mother to her son, and shook his head.

'Oh lassie . . . lassie . . .' He was an old man, remembering old sorrows. Wat, young and strong, laid a sheltering arm around his shoulders.

The others turned away, leaving them to their private thoughts, and crowded round Thomas anxious and questioning. But the Seannachie was not be drawn.

'Seek not to know that which does not concern you,' he said firmly. 'This only I will say. There are those who must do, and those who may know. You have done – almost – that which was required. The rest is for me to know, and for Gibbie to learn hereafter.'

'That lad is kin to Soulis,' snarled a voice. 'There's bad blood.'

'Aye right enough, and rode with him.'

A few of the men of Liddesdale who had seen Gibbie around the castle stepped forward menacingly. Thomas placed himself in front of the boy and raised a hand for silence.

'Rode with him it may be. But not for him.'

Marion slipped from Wat's grasp and stepped

forward to Gibbie's side.

'He brought me trust, and hope,' she said. 'Where there was no other.'

'And sought help where only he knew how!' Wat joined her, on the other side of the boy. The Seannachie stepped back and turned to face Gibbie, who bowed low as before a master.

'You will harm not a hair on his head, my lords,' he commanded, 'for he has the gift of vision. I have seen that this boy carries within him the blessing and the curse of the Old Knowledge. I will teach him to use that knowledge for good, to see still further, and to learn to read that which he sees.

'It may be that the day will come when you will have great need of him. Until then he is mine.'

'Keep him then, in safety and in peace,' said Wat grasping the Seannachie's hand. 'And know that you shall have my protection against any who dares threaten you.' He glared round the men who stood before them.

'And mine too!' The duke echoed him.

'Indeed, sirs, I thank you.' Thomas inclined his head towards them. 'But now − all is not yet over. Have no fear, Soulis is dead, but in order that you may live, you and your children in peace, the Doom must be fulfilled.'

He stood then with his back to the still smoking walls of Hermitage, raising his arms over the body of Ranulf de Soulis.

'Our chosen King Robert, by the Grace of God, Sovereign of this land and Overlord of the Isles, has cast him a curse upon this evil being.'

To each man who had been present in the King's Council Chamber at Ayr, came Robert's words, roaring in fury.

'Ye can boil him if you will – but trouble me no more.'

The words of a king. A curse pronounced which must be fulfilled. They drew back then, knowing what had to be done, but fearing even to touch the lifeless body.

Thomas read the thoughts in their minds.

'Iron cannot hurt him, nor rope hang, nor fire burn – even in death. So potent his power it is still to be feared indeed.'

'Then tell us what we must do,' demanded Wat. 'And let us be done with it now.'

'Strip the lead from the ruined roofs of Hermitage and bind Soulis in a winding sheet. Through lead the evil spirit may not pass. That done you must search the castle and bring to me the largest cauldron to be found.'

He turned from them then, with a dismissive wave of his hand, and sat on a fallen tree trunk, beckoning Gibbie to come to him.

Wat, his father and the others did as he ordered. In the gathering darkness they lit torches and entered the castle of Hermitage.

They clambered over fallen stones in the

courtyard, and in the antechamber where the steps to the dungeon lay buried deep in rubble. They searched through empty rooms with stifling dust and smoke heavy in the air. They hauled down sheets of lead, torn from shattered rooftops. In the kitchen where men lay dead upon the floor and the central hearth-fire of the castle still smouldered, they found a huge iron cauldron, black with age and fire. Dragging it from the rubble they carried it to the foot of the oak tree.

The Seannachie had them spread the sheets of lead on the grass beside Soulis. Seeing that in their superstition they feared even to approach the body, he himself stepped forward. Lifting him gently, he laid Ranulf de Soulis in his last winding sheet.

In the ring of light cast by their torches he laid the long fine hands, one on the other, across his chest. He softly closed the lids on those dark terror-filled eyes, and brushed back the tangled black hair. He turned the body on its side, drawing up the knees and bowing the head. Soulis lay like a child asleep, huddling close against nightmare and the unknown dark.

Thomas stood for a second, then with a sigh and a shake of the head he stepped back and allowed them to wrap the lead around the body and hammer it tightly down.

'How small,' thought Marion. 'How small he

seems in death, who filled the world with his presence in life.'

The Seannachie called to them to follow him and, leaning on Gibbie's shoulder, he set off into the trees.

'Bring me the body and the cauldron, and fetch kindling for we must set our fire by the Nine-Stane Rig.'

They staggered behind, following the light of his torch through the trees, dragging between them the body of Soulis and the great iron cauldron. On and upwards the Seannachie plodded, neither waiting for them nor breaking his step. Stumbling over tree roots, slithering on damp moss, they struggled to keep up with him, breaking branches as they passed to fill the cauldron with firewood.

They climbed at last, through thinning stunted trees to a high moorland where little grew, save heather and the bitter blaeberry, and where the wind moaned day and night. Beneath them stretched the sweep of Liddesdale, dark and silent. Not a candle burned in cottage or farmhouse to light their dead lord on his last and longest journey.

Across the dale, far to the east, the faint silvering of dawn broke through the windswept banks of cloud. The Seannachie paused, and the first chill breath of Autumn, blowing cold and fresh from the north, filled his robe, lifting it high behind him. He raised his right arm, pointing onward and upwards to those that followed him.

High on the top of that bleak moorland, stark against the greying sky, stood a ring of ancient standing stones. The Nine-Stane Rig.

Battered by rain and wind, baked by the suns of countless summers, and old as time itself, they had stood, a monument to man's worship of the Earth from which they were hewn, a symbol of everlasting strength. Eight massive columns of craggy stone about a fallen slab that lay like a broken altar at their heart.

Striding out strongly, Thomas led them towards the stones. Gibbie, clutching the casket, followed in his steps. Wat, supporting and encouraging Marion and the others, led them on. They were weary now, pausing to lay down their burdens, and then trudging doggedly on.

In the heart of the ring, where the vast flat stone lay split as if by some gargantuan hammer-blow, Thomas had them build a fire.

On top of the piled wood they placed the cauldron, and in it laid the lead-encased body of Soulis.

'Wood and water,' chanted the Seannachie, lifting his voice to the skies. 'Wood and water. Gift of the Earth, Gift of the Heavens.'

He had them fetch water from a moorland stream, filling helmets and water bottles until there was enough to cover the body.

119

Thomas waved them back and nodded to Gibbie to step forward. He lifted from around the boy's neck the pendant that he had worn since birth, the mark of evil and badge of the great House of Soulis.

He held it high, twisting in the watery light, then laid his fingertips on Gibbie's forehead, stroking gently as if drawing from him pain and grief for all time. The boy's face cleared and his dark eyes shone bright and warm.

Into his hands the Seannachie placed the pendant.

'Now Gilbert de Soulis, Lord of Liddesdale, now I charge you. To wood and water, gift of the Earth, gift of the Heavens, give fire, gift of the gods! Light you the flame of Freedom.'

Gibbie hurled the pendant deep into the heart of the brushwood. It glowed, then flared suddenly, blue and spitting. Sparks leapt from it catching the dry tinder. The flames spread fast and with a blinding white intensity, as though a gale raged through a forest fire.

As the water boiled, and the first steam rose wisping from the cauldron, the sun broke through the clouds, casting the shadow of the ring of stones around them, spreading a glow of comfort through their shivering bodies.

'Take thou thy evil with thee, and here endeth the story . . .' murmured Thomas the Seannachie, his eyes dreaming blue and distant as the heather-covered hills.

## Twelve

*And here endeth the story*

The full harvest moon hung like a glowing peach in the dark velvet sky above Branxholm. Music, light and laughter spilled from every wide open door and window of the old tower, as they had all day.

In the orchard by the river, moonlight sparkled on dew-damp grass. The leaves tossed in their sleep, tickled by a passing whisper of wind.

Wat and Marion slipped unnoticed from the hall to share a stolen moment of peace.

Beneath the overhanging branches of an old apple tree, hidden from the tower, they kissed. Wat slid down against the trunk to sit on the grass, pulling Marion gently into his lap. The quietness of the night settled around them. She lay stroking his hair, then ran a finger-tip down his forehead, tracing the line of the scar that would always be there.

'What are you thinking, Wat?'

'Mmmmm?'

'You look as if you're off with the Wee Folk. What is it, love?'

'Och – nothing. Whigmaleeries. Nonsense!' He caught her round the waist, hugging her tight as if suddenly afraid she might vanish, and buried his face in her hair.

'Wheesht, love,' she murmured. 'There's none can harm us. We're safe now.'

'Aye so we are. Safe – and married, Mistress Scott.' They kissed again, slow and sweet, then he pulled back and gazed at her shining eyes in the moonlight.

'I must be out of my mind,' he whispered softly. 'There'll never be another minute's peace to be had in this world . . .'

'Wat Scott! You great . . .'

'Wat! Marion! Where are you?' Allan has missed them. 'I can hear you. I know you're out there.' He paused, catching Marion's stifled giggle and the rustle of her skirt.

'Shhhhhh,' whispered Wat putting a finger to Marion's lips.

'I'll count up to a hundred and then I'll find you. I'm coming!

*"Come out, come out wherever you are,*
*The bogey man's come tae find ye."* '

He chanted the old game the three of them had played so often as children.

'Come on back in. The Seannachie has promised us a last story before he leaves. You'll miss the fun.'

He fumbled down the dark path, silhouetted in the golden light from the doorway, and tripped with a noisy clatter over a basket full of windfallen apples.

'What fool left that there?'

Wat laughed and rolled to his feet, pulling Marion with him.

'Mistress Scott, I fear we'd best take your drunken brother home before he kills himself.'

'Your brother, too, now – husband. Come on, we can share the daft beggar between us.'

They heaved Allan to his feet, straightened his tunic and, linking arms, went laughing up the path. Wrapped in their own glow of happiness the three entered the hall together, blinking in the light.

'A reel, a reel! A wedding reel for the bride and groom!' The duke thumped the table. His cry was picked up by the guests, the chant grew louder, the musicians joined in, and Wat and Marion were swept into the mad whirligig of clapping, stamping colour.

Later, resting, Marion watched the company. Her mother sat, beaming, at the top table, her plump fingers tapping to the music, her round homely face shining and rosy as an apple above the pink velvet. Her father, uncomfortably splendid in a new robe, sat with the duke. The two heads nodded close together, deep in talk of

123

land and beasts no doubt, and the price of corn.

'Aye, man it was a good harvest, but I've seen better mind.'

Good farmers and countrymen both of them!

Her father was the proudest man there this day, no doubt of that. Proud to see his daughter so finely married. She smoothed a hand down the skirt of the heavy yellow silk gown. It had been a gift from the king, that and the jewels she now wore about her neck. He only was missing from the wedding feast, brooding at Ayr, sick and alone. It was said by those closest to him that he had taken the news of the death of Ranulf de Soulis badly, seeing in it blame only for himself, a further burden to his troubled conscience.

But few thought of him this day – or of Soulis.

A shout caught her attention. Allan led the fun, fast and furious, joining in a song here, spinning a pretty girl off her feet there. He seemed almost demented in his determination to whip the fun to a frenzy and keep it there, as if the laughter must somehow be more intense for having followed what went before.

Before. Marion shivered at the memory. Wat, returning to her side, sensed her mood and caught her hands in his, warm and comforting. Where Allan was wilder, Wat seemed to have become quieter, but he had grown in strength and authority. It was to him that the king would turn in future.

The music whirled to a finish. Dancers spun rosy-faced from the floor to find a seat and a stoup of wine.

'Hush! Silence for the Seannachie. Sit down there, you daft limmer!'

The servants dragged forward an old heavy chair and placed it in the centre of the hall. Thomas rose from his seat at the top table by the side of Marion's mother. Silence fell around him.

'Wheesht now. It's time for a tale.'

'Pit doon that lass, Allan Elliot, and behave yourself.'

Gradually silence fell on the company. Dancers who had skirled through reel after reel settled peacefully. Children who had fallen asleep in dark corners woke and crept to their mother's sides. The servants, still scrubbing and polishing in the kitchen, left the pots and pans and tiptoed up to sit on the stairs and listen.

The duke banged a huge fist on the table, calling for quiet, and all eyes turned to the tall man in the faded blue robe.

Thomas the Seannachie gazed deep into the fire a moment longer, as if seeking there the story he was about to tell. A twig snapped in the flames, throwing out a tiny shower of sparks. Thomas turned in his chair, the strange blue eyes lifted, and he began the tale.

'Now come all you, from far and near, and hark to what I say . . .'

It was an old tale of love and evil, of courage and fear, of fights lost and friendships won.

Dreaming, Marion's mind floated free with the words.

'. . . then take thou thy evil with thee – and here endeth the story,' declaimed Thomas the Seannachie, his eyes dreaming and distant.

Returning as if from a far-off world beyond moon and stars, Marion saw again the faces about her in the old familiar hall of Branxholm Tower.

She lingered on those she loved. Her father and mother, Allan, the old duke – and Wat, who was now and forever by her side. Each sat quiet, filled with their own thoughts.

'. . . and here endeth the story . . .'

The silence fell, golden still with the echo of the Seannachie's voice.

Deep in the woods beyond Branxholm, half-heard above the chuckle of the river, a lone magpie called in the night.

By the fireside, head bowed on his arms, Gibbie sat cradling the precious casket.